U0046418

under the weather

✕ 天氣之下　○ 身體不適

Shadowing 跟讀

Lora ── 著　　阿譯 ── 譯

100+句 學校沒教 的英文慣用語

秒讚口說考官高分表達・躍升母語程度 English Speaker

a rain check

✕ 雨天支票　○ 改天再約

crack me up

✕ 使我破裂　○ 笑掉大牙

音檔
使用說明

STEP ❶

掃描書中 QRCode

STEP ❷

快速註冊或登入 EZCourse

STEP ❸

請回答以下問題完成訂閱

一、請問本書第65頁，紅色框線中的英
文＿＿＿＿是什麼？

二、請問本書第33頁，紅色框線中的英
文＿＿＿＿是什麼？

答案　請注意大小寫

送出

回答問題按送出

答案就在書中（需注意空格與大小寫）。

STEP ❹

完成訂閱

該書右側會顯示「已訂閱」，
表示已成功訂閱，
即可點選播放本書音檔。

STEP ❺

點選個人檔案

查看「我的訂閱紀錄」
會顯示已訂閱本書，
點選封面可到本書線上聆聽。

學英文講求一種「Feel」！

但要怎麼做才能把英文學好呢？

如果想要自然地用英文對話，就要避免直接把中文翻成英文，而是學習英文母語者慣用的表達法。比起艱澀的單字，英文母語者更常用慣用語 (idioms) 和片語動詞 (phrasal verbs) 來表達自己的意思。如果光知道很多單字，卻不懂得運用慣用語及片語動詞的話，不但很難確切理解母語者所說的話，說英文也無法達到母語者的境界。

語言反映著文化與生活，因此本書將從美國文化、慣用語、俚語、會話文法，及台灣人容易犯的錯誤對症下藥。打破傳統文法、會話分科學習，將文法實際融入生活會話中，讓你講英文就像母語人士自然流利。

本書的所有表達方式，都是我在加州生活十幾年，就讀小學到大學，美國人真正會說的道地表達法，將 10 年來的知識經驗完整集結於本書中。

希望英文帶給大家的不是壓力，而是幸福感。我也期待看到各位透過學習英文飛得更高更遠，用英文這個溝通工具結下更多良緣。也祝福各位健康平安。

祝福各位擁有比今天更美好的明天。

Lora

STUDY GUIDE
學習方式

今日慣用語

英文母語者日常生活中經常使用的慣用語！

Let's Learn!

學習對話中的文法、句型、諺語、流行俚語、美式文化，並糾正常見台式英文錯誤。

Give someone the benefit of the doubt
姑且相信某人

法律上沒有證據確定被告是否有罪時，疑點（doubt）與利益（benefit）歸於被告，採無罪推定原則。應用於日常生活中時，則可以解釋為雖然心裡有所懷疑，但是在有心證卻沒有物證的情況下，還是姑且先相信對方。

Teddy	So Sorry! I was stuck in a very heavy traffic jam.
Jade	You are late again. Last time you said your car broke down.
Teddy	I know it doesn't make sense but you need to give me the benefit of the doubt.
Jade	Three times in a row but fine I'll give you the benefit of the doubt. But this has gotta be your last time.
Teddy	Argh! This is so frustrating. I wish I could prove it to you!

泰迪	抱歉！我因為塞車被困住了。
潔德	你又遲到了。你上次説你的車壞掉。
泰迪	我知道這樣很扯，但妳不能直接有罪推定。
潔德	你已經連續三次了。算了，我就姑且相信你，但這次是最後一次。
泰迪	吼！我也很無奈，真希望有證據可以證明給妳看！

情境對話

將慣用語、道地口說表達融入實用的生活對話中。

EXPRESSION **get/be stuck in a traffic jam**

stuck（動彈不得的）in traffic jam（在塞車中）的意思是「因塞車而動彈不得」。

EXPRESSION **It doesn't make sense**

面對無法理解，或不合理的狀況時可以使用的這句話。相反地，表示情況説得通、合理，則用 It makes sense。

Do you think this makes sense?
你覺得這樣合理嗎？

SPOKEN ENGLISH **Gotta**

have got to 的縮寫，have to~ 是「必須～」的意思。母語者説話時會省略 have，got to 連音為 gotta。

I gotta go. 我要走了。	**You gotta eat healthy.** 你要吃健康一點。

MOST CONFUSED **wish vs. hope**

wish 用於「不可能實現」或「幾乎不可能發生」的願望，hope 用於「真心期盼會實現」的願望。但是「wish + 名詞」時，相同於 hope 的意思。

I wish I were taller. 真希望我能長得高一點。
▸ 成人再長高的機率微乎其微，所以是用與現在事實相反的假設語氣，用過去式 were。

I hope you get well soon! 希望你快點好起來！
▸ 真心希望對方快點康復。

We wish you a Merry Christmas! 我們祝你聖誕快樂！
▸〈wish + 名詞〉同 hope「真心期盼」之意。

wish	hope
I wish you had a good time. 我真希望你能玩得開心一點。 ▸ 事實上玩得不開心	**I hope you have a good time.** 我祝你玩得愉快。

Day 9

STEP 1　**先聽 MP3 檔案再看書**

先聽完對話音檔後，閱讀並解析本文內容。
● Let's Learn! 的部分也都要讀喔。

STEP 2　**Shadowing 影子練習**

以一句或一行為區間，反覆播放 MP3 音檔，聽完一句話後按暫停 ▷||，講出聽到的句子，一直重複到熟練為止。接著配合音檔練習「同步跟讀」。每天針對當天的對話反覆練習「聽後跟讀」和「同步跟讀」。

Let's Practice!

每十日複習計畫，透過練習題驗收是否確實記住慣用語。

Let's Practice!
DAY 11-20

Exercise 1 請用題目中給的單字造句。

1. 這真的好煩！（pain）
_____

2. 珍妮背叛了我！（stab）
_____

3. 我請客！（on）
_____

4. 保持平常心，持續前進。（Keep calm）
_____

5. 振作！（put）
_____

6. 真的好久不見！（ages）
_____

7. 像個男子漢！（man）
_____

8. 我在家耍廢。（veg）
_____

9. 一切都水到渠成。（fall into）
_____

10. 你喜歡什麼樣的男人？（go for）
_____

解答 1
1) This is pain in the ass! 2) Jenny stabbed me in the back! 3) It's on me! 4) Keep calm and carry on. 5) Put yourself together! 6) It's been ages! 7) Man up! 8) I vegged out at home.
9) Everything fell into place. 10) What kind of guy do you go for?

Exercise 2 依照句意填入正確答案。

1. 我最近沒錢。
I'm _____ these days.
2. 報應是很可怕的。
_____ is a _____.
3. 要不要一起看 Netflix 耍廢？
Do you wanna _____?
4. 他露出他的本色。
He _____ his _____.
5. 你吃錯藥哦？
What has _____?
6. 我是過來人。
_____and done that.
7. 內在美更重要。
_____ is only skin deep.
8. 我討厭週一症候群。
I hate _____.
9. 羅馬不是一天造成的。
_____ built in _____.
10. 人生不會照著計畫進行。
_____ happens.

解答 2
1) broke 2) Karma, bitch 3) Netflix and chill 4) revealed, true colors 5) gotten into you
6) Been there 7) Beauty 8) Monday blues 9) Rome was not, a day 10) Life

---

STEP 3　**只看解析，然後用英文說出來**

試著一邊看解析，一邊說出英文句子。如果想不太起來，就檢查一下英文對話。反覆練習到只要看解析，就可以流利說出當天的對話全文為止。

STEP 4　**回答練習題**

透過練習題再次確認是否確實吸收了十天之間所學的內容。

STUDY PLAN

學習計畫

STUDY PLAN

學習計畫

STUDY PLAN

學習計畫

Let's Practice
練習題

Get outta here!
在供蝦米肖威！別搞笑了好嗎！

如果你以為 Get outta here! 只是「滾出去！」，那就得專心看下去囉。在美國 Get outta here! 還有「在説什麼東西！」、「開什麼玩笑？」、「別搞笑了好嗎！」等涵義，與 You've got to be kidding me. 相似，但是語氣更強烈。原句是 Get out of here.，母語人士習慣把 want to 唸成 wanna，going to 唸成 gonna，也會將 out of 連音成 outta。因此，連音是聽懂母語者、提升口説流利度的關鍵。

Justin	Have you heard? Chris Evans and Lily James are going out!
Lora	💬 **Get outta here!** I don't buy that crap.
Justin	No, for real! It's everywhere on the internet.
Lora	You've got to be kidding me! Chris is the love of my life! He is my Captain!
Justin	Psh. Wake up and smell the coffee. He is a star, not your Prince Charming.

賈斯汀	妳聽説了嗎？美國隊長克里斯伊凡和英國演員莉莉詹姆斯在交往！
蘿拉	少在那邊！我才不相信。
賈斯汀	不，是真的！網路上消息都出來了！
蘿拉	怎麼可能！克里斯永遠都是我的！他是屬於我的隊長！
賈斯汀	噗，妳醒醒吧。他是大明星，不是妳的白馬王子。

SLANG I don't buy the crap.

buy 除了「買」的意思外，也有「相信，接受」的意思。I don't buy it. 是「我才不相信」，等同於 I don't believe it。crap 有「大便」的意思，所以 I don't buy the crap. 就是「我才不信那種鬼話」的意思。

Do you buy that?
你相信嗎？

Don't buy that!
別信！

EXPRESSION You've got to be kidding me!

You've got to be kidding! / You kidding! / Are you kidding? / You are kidding me! 可以在無言以對的狀況下，表示「開什麼玩笑？」、「太扯了」等意思。kidding 也可以用 joking 來替換。

EXCLAMATION Psh.

對某事感到無奈或是不同意對方意見時可以做出的反應，但也可能顯得失禮，使用上要注意。

Psh! Shut up!
噗！不要搞笑好嗎！

IDIOM Wake up and smell the coffee.

想叫那些滿腦子白日夢、不切實際的人清醒點？就跟他說「醒來聞聞咖啡的味道」。

Wake up and smell the coffee! The reality is cruel.
清醒點吧！現實是很殘酷的。

EXPRESSION Prince Charming

戲劇中經常出現帥氣迷人的「白馬王子」，用英文說就是 Prince Charming。這個用法也有出現在 1950 年的迪士尼動畫《仙履奇緣》中。

He is my Prince Charming!
他是我的白馬王子！

Grass is always greener on the other side

吃碗內，看碗外；外國的月亮比較圓

「另一邊的草總是比較綠」，也就是「別人碗裡的東西看起來特別好吃」的
意思。不容易從自己的生活中獲得滿足，這種感覺不分東、西方，任何人都
會有。當身邊的人對生活有所抱怨，或是將自己與他人做比較而感到心情低
落時，就告訴他「Grass is always greener on the other side」吧。

Teddy	What's up? Why the long face?
Kathy	Everyone on social media seems happy. Everyone has a perfect life.
Teddy	It's social media!
Kathy	I know, but I'm going through a hard time and I can't help thinking negative.
Teddy	You gotta remember, " 💬 **Grass is always greener on the other side.**"

泰迪	妳怎麼了？為什麼一副苦瓜臉？
凱西	社群媒體上大家都看起來好快樂，每個人都過得比我好。
泰迪	社群媒體本來就是這樣啊！
凱西	我知道，但是我最近過得不太好，沒辦法控制自己的負面思考。
泰迪	別忘了，「外國的月亮比較圓」大家只會羨慕別人。

SLANG **What's up?**

What's up? 可以當作 How are you? 打招呼用語，也經常用來表示「怎麼回事？」或「幹嘛這樣？」的意思。拼法有 Wazzup? / Wassup? / Waddup?，也可以縮讀為 'Sup?。

What's up? Is something wrong?
怎麼了？有什麼問題嗎？

IDIOM **Why the long face?**

可別以為別人是在說「臉為什麼那麼長？」，這句俚語是用來詢問對方「為什麼看起來鬱鬱寡歡的？」或是「為什麼看起來有什麼不滿？」。

Why the long face? You look like you are gonna burst into tears.
為什麼一臉難過的樣子？你看起來快哭了。

GRAMMAR **Everyone seems happy**

everyone、everybody 後面要接「單數動詞」，every 接「單數名詞 + 單數動詞」。

Everyone has a perfect life.
大家都有完美的生活。

Everybody looks happy on Instagram.
Instagram 上所有人看起來都好快樂。

Everything is so tasty!
什麼都好吃！

Every single person regardless of gender, age and race needs to be respected.
無論性別、年齡、種族，每個人都應該受到尊重。

TAIGLISH **IG 是台式英文！**

雖然 Instagram 縮寫 IG，但英文母語者習慣說 Insta ／ the Gram。Facebook 縮寫 FB，但是外國人只會完整說出全名 Facebook。因此不要再說「哀居」、「F 逼」了！

MOST MISTAKEN **「我最近過得好累」用英文怎麼說？**

有用過 I'm hard. 說自己過得很辛苦的人請舉手。在我聽過的錯誤裡，沒有什麼比這更令人傻眼了。hard 的確可以用來表示「困難的、辛苦的」，但可別忘了它也有「硬的」意思。所以 I'm hard. 其實是「我硬了」，這可說是最尷尬的錯誤了。正確的說法：I'm going through a very difficult time (in my life). 也可以用 I've been going through tough/rough times.。

Slow and steady wins the race
沉穩踏實者終將得勝

一路長銷的商品稱為「steady seller」，steady 的意思是「穩定的」。因此這句諺語就是在説「只要穩定不停地邁進，終將會在比賽中獲勝」。最近有時會看到「一個月就能開口説」、「只要三個月，月薪就能變成一般上班族的年薪」等英文教學廣告文案，但世上沒什麼是可以不勞而獲的，慢慢來也沒關係，堅持下去才是最重要的。

Alex	I've been looking for a job for months but nobody wants to hire me.
Rachel	It must be so hard. I'm sorry to hear that.
Alex	I'm losing self-confidence.
Rachel	Put your chin up! Just keep doing what you've been doing. I believe in you.
Alex	Thanks for saying that.
Rachel	No matter what you do, 💬 **slow and steady wins the race!**

艾力克斯	我一直在找工作，但都沒有地方要用我。
瑞秋	辛苦你了，聽你這麼説我也很難過。
艾力克斯	我越來越沒有自信了。
瑞秋	振作點！堅持下去繼續找吧，我相信你。
艾力克斯	謝謝妳的鼓勵。
瑞秋	不管做什麼，只要穩紮穩打一定會成功的！

MOST CONFUSED look for vs. find

look for 和 find 的差異是台灣人常搞混的問題之一。兩者都是「找」，不過 look for 指「尋找的過程」，而 find 則是「找到的結果」。

I'm looking for my phone.
我在找我的手機。（過程）

I found my phone!
我找到手機了！（結果）

Who are you looking for?
你在找誰？（過程）

Did you find it?
你找到了嗎？（結果）

EXPRESSION I'm sorry to hear that.

這句話不是在道歉，而是在說「聽到這個消息，讓我感到很遺憾」。I'm sorry. 是英文中常見的反應句，想要表達「哎呀」、「怎麼辦」等的情緒，可以加上 Oh no! 。

IDIOM Put your chin up!

直譯的話就是「抬起下巴！」，也就是「有自信點！」、「挺起胸膛！」、「加油！」的意思。

Put your chin up! You are glorious!
有自信點！你很棒！

PATTERN keep (on) + 動名詞

用來表示某件事持續發生，或持續進行某行動。

He kept on talking.
他一直說個不停。

It keeps on snowing.
一直在下雪。

MOST CONFUSED believe vs. believe in

believe 單純相信，判斷真假；believe in 信任（某人、能力）或信念（可能存在）。

Please believe me!
請相信我！

Please believe in me.
請對我有信心。

I believe him.
我相信他！

I believe in God.
我相信神的存在。

04

Everything happens for a reason
事出必有因

人生總有一些不如意的事，例如深愛的人離開自己，或是無法實現真心渴望的夢想。然而這所有的經驗都是成就今日我們的養分。失去過深愛的人，才更懂得對新對象心懷感謝；因為無法實現夢想，才學會保持謙虛。發生在我們生命中的一切都是有原因的。

Logan　Hi Esther, I heard you broke up with Kyle.
　　　　Are you OK?

Esther　I guess we weren't meant to be.

Logan　Well, I believe 💬 **everything happens for a reason**.

Esther　I would like to believe so.

Logan　Hang in there, girl. Time will heal.

Esther　Thanks for calling!

羅根　　嗨，伊絲特。聽說妳跟凱爾分手了，妳還好嗎？

伊絲特　我想我跟他注定無緣。

羅根　　我相信凡事都是有原因的。

伊絲特　我也告訴自己要這麼想。

羅根　　加油吧，時間是最好的解藥。

伊絲特　謝謝你打給我。

MOST CONFUSED **hear vs. listen**

hear 是指偶然聽聞訊息、傳言、聲音等傳入「耳朵」的情況，listen 則是有意識地、專注地、主動地用「心裡的耳朵」去傾聽。

Have you heard the news?
你有聽說那個消息嗎？

Are you listening?
你有在聽嗎？

MOST MISTAKEN **break 是「斷裂，破碎」**

有些人會說 I broke my boyfriend/girlfriend. 什麼？怎麼會把男友／女友折斷呢？動詞 break 後面一定要接介系詞 up (with) 才能表示「（和某人）分手」的意思。一句話的語意會因為介系詞的不同而有很大的差別，要多留意。

break out 事件爆發	**The Korean War <u>broke out</u> on June 25, 1950.** 韓戰爆發於 1950 年 6 月 25 日。
break in(to) 闖入	**Someone <u>broke into</u> my car and stole my gum!** 有人闖進我的車，偷走我的口香糖！
break down 故障；崩潰	**I <u>broke down</u> and cried like a baby.** 我崩潰了，哭得像個小孩一樣。
break away 逃脫、獨立	**I want to <u>break away</u> from my bad habits.** 我想要擺脫我的壞習慣。

IDIOM **meant to be**

It is meant to be. 是指某件事是「注定的」。稱讚相配的情侶時可以說 You guys are so meant to be together.「你們是天生一對」，也就是「很速配」的意思。

IDIOM **Hang in there ！**

什麼叫「吊在那裡」？其實這是告訴對方「雖然很辛苦，但再撐一下，加把勁」。

Hang in there! Everything's gonna be all right.
再努力一下！一切都會沒事的。

IDIOM **Time will heal.**

時間會治好一切，也就是「時間是最好的解藥」的意思。痛苦或悲傷都會被時間沖淡。

Time heals!

Time is the best medicine.

時間能治癒一切。

時間是最好的解藥。

It is what it is
不然能怎麼辦？

曾有人問美國前總統川普：「為何你不勸自己的支持者戴口罩？」他回答：「They are dying. It's true but it is what it is.」對此事表示了「許多生命正在消逝是事實，但事情就是這樣，不然能怎麼辦？」的意見。在過得不太順心時，告訴自己 It is what it is. 既然無法改變，那就換個心境好好面對吧。

Mason   I'm feeling super frustrated with this whole COVID-19 pandemic!

Diane   I feel ya. I also had to cancel my trip to Paris.

Mason   Sigh. I wonder when this would all end.

Diane   Well, 💬 **it is what it is**. Life goes on.

Mason   True. I guess we just need to accept it.

Diane   It sucks so much, though.

梅森   我快被 COVID-19 疫情逼瘋了！

黛安   我懂，我的巴黎之旅也被迫取消了。

梅森   唉，到底疫情什麼時候才會結束？

黛安   嗯，能怎麼辦呢？日子還是要過。

梅森   沒錯，我們只能接受現實。

黛安   但是真的好煩唷。

MOST ASKED　frustrated 不只是「挫敗的」

frustrated 還有「煩悶的」意思，狀況不順心、思緒複雜、內心煩悶的時候，就可以說 I'm frustrated. 若是因為空間狹窄而感到窒悶，則要用 stuffy 或 suffocating 來表示。

EXPRESSION　I feel ya.

I feel you. 不是「我感覺到你」，而是「有共鳴、我懂你的感受」的意思。母語使用者口語上經常把 you 發音成 ya，也會把 you all（你們所有人）連音成 y'all。

MOST CONFUSED　trip vs. travel

trip 通常使用「名詞」，travel 常用「動詞」型態。很多人自我介紹都會說 I love travel.，這是錯誤用法，喜歡旅行正確的說法是 I love <u>to</u> travel. 或 I love travel<u>ing</u>.，一句話不能同時出現兩個動詞，travel 要用「to 不定詞」或「動名詞」來表示。如果想用 trip 這個名詞來表達喜歡旅行的話，則可以說 I love going on trips.

EXPRESSION　Life goes on.

意指「不管遇到什麼考驗，人生都在繼續向前進」。只要還活著，人生就不會停下來。推薦大家聽聽看美國西岸饒舌代表性人物「2Pac」的歌曲《Life Goes On》。

Get up and broaden your shoulders because no matter what life goes on!
抬頭挺胸振作起來，不管發生什麼事，人生都在繼續！

SLANG　It sucks!

可以用在各種不同的情況，表達「好煩！」、「好爛！」、「不怎麼樣！」、「好可惜！」等各種心情的俚語。而要表示自己不善於某事的時候，則加介系詞 at。

I suck at cooking.
我很不會做菜。

It sucks that I can't see you today.
真可惜今天沒見到你。

You can't go wrong with it
絕對錯不了

直譯的話是「你不會有錯」，也就是「絕對不可能失敗」、「絕對不會出錯」的意思。You can't go wrong with 後面也可以接 sb/sth。想更進一步強調，則可以加上 never，You can NEVER go wrong with it!

You can NEVER go wrong with "Thank you."
經常把「謝謝」掛嘴邊是絕不會出錯的好習慣。

Sis	I'm starving to death! Let's go grab a bite!
Bro	I haven't eaten all day, too. What do you want?
Sis	I'm craving meat.
Bro	💬 **You can't go wrong with** Korean BBQ!
Sis	My mouth is watering already. Let's bounce!

姐姐	我快餓死了，我們趕快去覓食！
弟弟	我也整天沒吃，妳想吃什麼？
姐姐	我想吃肉。
弟弟	那吃韓國烤肉就對了。
姐姐	光想就口水直流了，走吧！

EXPRESSION **to death**

to 有「朝～方向」的意思，這片語用來誇飾某種狀態到「～快死了」的程度。

I'm bored to death.
我快無聊死了。

I'm scared to death.
我快嚇死了。

SLANG **Let's go grab a bite!**

表示「去吃點什麼吧」的俚語。主要用在三明治或貝果等簡便輕食。也可說 Let's go grab something to eat.

Do you wanna go grab a bite?
要不要去吃點小東西？

EXPRESSION **crave**

表示強烈渴望某事物，想要說「我超想吃」特定食物時，就可以說 I crave (something).

What do you crave?
你想吃什麼？

I'm craving pizza right now.
我現在超想吃披薩。

IDIOM **My mouth is watering.**

指受到美食誘惑，口水直流。mouthwatering 用來形容食物好吃「令人垂涎三尺的」。

It looks mouthwatering!
那看起來好好吃！

SLANG **bounce**

雖然是「彈跳」的意思，不過在口語中可以當作 go，代表「走」或「離開」。

I'm gonna bounce. See you tomorrow, guys.
我要閃了，大家明天見啦。

It's no use crying over spilt milk
覆水難收

直譯是「為已經打翻的牛奶哭泣沒意義」，表示「別留戀過去」、「覆水難收」。有時回想起自己曾經做錯的選擇，內心難免會感到難受。我為什麼那麼做？我為什麼沒有挽留他？我那時為何要發火？早知道當初就不要投資那筆錢了！然而一切都已成為過去，現在後悔只是浪費時間。有時間後悔，不如想想該如何補救過去犯下的錯。

Sam　I shouldn't have entered this company from the get-go.

Nick　Oh, please! There you go again!

Sam　I should've majored in something else in college.

Nick　💬 **It's no use crying over spilt milk!**
Everything you are talking about is spilt milk.

Sam　Sorry.

Nick　What's done is done. Let's just booze away sorrows!

珊姆　早知道就不要進這間公司了。

尼克　吼，好了啦！你又來了！

珊姆　我大學應該選別的系才對。

尼克　覆水難收！妳現在說這些都沒有用。

珊姆　抱歉。

尼克　事已成定局。我們去喝一杯忘掉煩惱吧！

GRAMMAR I should (not) have + p.p.

✦ **I should have + p.p.** （過去應該要～）
表達過去應該做，卻沒有做。

I should have studied harder.
早知道就認真讀書了。

I should have told you.
我應該要告訴你才對。

✦ **I shouldn't have + p.p.** （過去不應該～）
表達過去不應該做，卻做了。

I shouldn't have slacked off.
早知道就不要偷懶了。

I shouldn't have screamed at you.
我不該對你大小聲。

SLANG from the get-go

get-go 是「最一開始」的意思。也寫作 git-go，原是非裔美國人使用的俚語。

I didn't like it from the get-go!
我從一開始就不喜歡！

I've known it from the get-go.
我從一開始就知道了。

IDIOM What's done is done.

直譯是「事情做了就做了」，表達「木已成舟」，事已成定局，無法改變過去。類似本課的 It's no use crying over spilt milk. 也可説 Don't dwell on the past. / Past is past. / It's water under the bridge. 等。

SLANG booze away sorrows

booze 是 alcohol 的俚語，可作為動詞或名詞。booze away 指「喝酒排解情緒」，sorrow 是悲傷，即「借酒澆愁」的意思。

I boozed away sorrows last night.
（動詞）
我昨天借酒澆愁。

I want some booze.
（名詞）
我想喝點酒。

 08

A leopard can't change its spots

牛牽到北京還是牛;江山易改本性難移

直譯是「花豹無法改變自己身上的花紋」,表示「我們無法修正一個人的個性」,但這句話不能說 You can't fix people.(你不能修理別人),導致語意不符。因此,說英文時,除了避免直譯,也要學習母語人士的表達方式。

Aaron　Do you believe people can change?

Lora　I actually believe 💬 **a leopard can't change its spots.** However, I also believe people can change by the power of love.

Aaron　Really? I find it hard to believe.

Lora　I had the luck to experience the power of love. But it takes time.

Aaron　For the love of God! Nothing comes easy!

亞倫　妳覺得人可以改變嗎?

蘿拉　我相信江山易改本性難移,不過我也認為愛的力量能夠改變一個人。

亞倫　真的嗎?我不太相信。

蘿拉　我很幸運,我曾經體會過愛的力量。但是這需要一點時間。

亞倫　吼唷!人生怎麼沒一件事是輕鬆的!

GRAMMAR 抽象名詞 power、luck、love 前面，為何加上了定冠詞「the」呢？

power、luck 還有 love 皆為不可數的抽象概念，前面不能使用冠詞。

不過對話中說到 power、luck 還有 love 時，前面卻加上了定冠詞「the」。the power of love 不是泛指抽象力量，而是明確指稱「愛帶來的那份力量」所以前方出現了定冠詞，同樣地 the luck to experience the power of love 句中的 luck 不是泛稱幸運，而是具體點出「有幸體會愛的力量」的「幸運」。最後，for the love of God 並非單指愛，而是確切指出「神的愛」。所以這些情況都一樣使用了定冠詞。同理，要記得根據文理及情況的不同，抽象名詞前面是有可能加上冠詞的！

PATTERN I find it hard to + 原形動詞

I find it hard to 是表示「很難～（做某事）」的句型。這裡的 find 不是「尋找」，而是「覺得」的意思。

I find it hard to say "No".
我很難拒絕別人。

I find it hard to get up in the morning.
我覺得早上起床好痛苦。

EXPRESSION For the love of God!

感到驚訝、憤怒時使用，可解釋為「天殺的」、「該死」、「吼唷」、「拜託」等意思。這個表達方式類似 for God's sake、oh my God!。

For the love of God, stop it!
吼，看在老天的份上，到此為止吧！

For the love of God, be careful!
哎呀，小心點！

For the love of God, hurry!
拜託你，動作快點！

EXPRESSION Nothing comes easy!

「凡事得來不易」，也就是「世上沒有不勞而獲的事」。

Nothing comes easy. You gotta work real hard for it.
凡事得來不易，努力耕耘才會有收穫。

Give someone the benefit of the doubt
姑且相信某人

法律上沒有證據確定被告是否有罪時，疑點（doubt）與利益（benefit）歸於被告，採無罪推定原則。應用於日常生活中時，則可以解釋為雖然心裡有所懷疑，但是在有心證卻沒有物證的情況下，還是姑且先相信對方。

Teddy   So Sorry! I was stuck in a very heavy traffic jam.

Jade   You are late again. Last time you said your car broke down.

Teddy   I know it doesn't make sense but you need to 💬 **give me the benefit of the doubt**.

Jade   Three times in a row but fine I'll give you the benefit of the doubt. But this has gotta be your last time.

Teddy   Argh! This is so frustrating. I wish I could prove it to you!

泰迪   抱歉！我因為塞車被困住了。

潔德   你又遲到了。你上次說你的車壞掉。

泰迪   我知道這樣很扯，但妳不能直接有罪推定。

潔德   你已經連續三次了。算了，我就姑且相信你，但這次是最後一次。

泰迪   吼！我也很無奈，真希望有證據可以證明給妳看！

EXPRESSION **get/be stuck in a traffic jam**

stuck（動彈不得的）in traffic jam（在塞車中）的意思是「因塞車而動彈不得」。

EXPRESSION **It doesn't make sense**

面對無法理解，或不合理的狀況時可以使用的這句話。相反地，表示情況説得通、合理，則用 It makes sense。

Do you think this makes sense?
你覺得這樣合理嗎？

SPOKEN ENGLISH **Gotta**

have got to 的縮讀，have to~ 是「必須～」的意思。母語者説話時會省略 have，got to 連音為 gotta。

I gotta go.
我要走了。

You gotta eat healthy.
你要吃得健康一點。

MOST CONFUSED **wish vs. hope**

wish 用於「不可能實現」或「幾乎不可能發生」的願望，hope 用於「真心期盼會實現」的願望。但是「wish + 名詞」時，相同於 hope 的意思。

I wish I were taller. 真希望我能長得高一點。

▶ 成人再長高的機率微乎其微，所以用與現在事實相反的假設語氣，用過去式 were。

I hope you get well soon! 希望你快點好起來！

▶ 真心希望對方快點康復。

We wish you a Merry Christmas! 我們祝你聖誕快樂！

▶〈wish + 名詞〉同 hope「真心期盼」之意。

<u>wish</u>

I wish you had a good time.
我真希望你能玩得開心一點。

▶ 事實上玩得不開心

<u>hope</u>

I hope you have a good time.
我祝你玩得愉快。

Where there is a will there is a way

有志者事竟成

will 是「意志」，儘管看似不可能實現，但只要有心就會找到方向，即「有志者事竟成」。國際大導李安研究所畢業後，曾失業長達六年，但他並未放棄電影生涯持續努力，最終獲得兩屆奧斯卡金像獎「最佳導演獎」，成為首度獲獎的亞洲導演，也是至今唯一兩度獲得該獎項的亞洲導演。

Johnson My dream is to be on the world stage.

Kendall No wonder you are so into learning English these days!

Johnson Correct. I'm all about studying English these days.

Kendall I strongly believe 💬 **where there is a will there is a way**.

Johnson I really appreciate your words and support. It means a lot to me.

強森 我的夢想是登上國際舞台。

坎朵 難怪你最近埋頭學英文！

強森 沒錯，我最近腦子裡除了念英文之外什麼都沒有。

坎朵 我相信有志者事竟成。

強森 謝謝妳的鼓勵，這對我來說很重要。

PATTERN **No wonder + (that) 子句**

No wonder 是表示「難怪！」的感嘆詞。後面可以接子句表達「難怪會那樣啊！」的意思。

No wonder you are so skinny! You barely eat.
難怪你這麼瘦！你幾乎不吃東西。

EXPRESSION **into (someone/something)**

形容人沉迷某事或為某人著迷。有一部知名小說就叫做《 He Is Not That Into You 他其實沒那麼喜歡妳》，也改編成同名電影，Check it out! （快去看看吧！）

I'm so into you.
我愛上你了。

What are you into these days?
你最近在迷什麼？

EXPRESSION **all about (something/someone)**

直譯為「全部都是（某事、某人）」，即在某人眼裡「只在乎某事、某人」。

I'm all about you.
你是我的一切。/ 我心裡只有你。/
除了你，我什麼都不在乎。

Lora is all about teaching English and her students.
蘿拉一心只想著英文教學和她的學生們。

EXPRESSION **It means a lot.**

mean 作動詞使用時是「意味著」的意思，作形容詞使用則有「刻薄的」、「壞的」等意思。It means a lot 是母語使用者常用的表達方式之一，意思是「這對我來說意義重大」，也就是「這帶給我很大的力量」。

It means the world to me!
（動詞）
這對我來說非常重要！

You are so mean!
（形容詞）
你真的很惡劣！

Let's Practice!
DAY 1-10

請用題目中給的單字造句。

1. 我不相信你說的話。（buy）

_____

2. 你怎麼一副苦瓜臉？（face）

_____

3. 我聽到消息，感到很遺憾。（hear）

_____

4. 我和男友分手了。（break）

_____

5. 我很不會做菜。（suck）

_____

6. 我超想吃肉。（crave）

_____

7. 早知道就不要偷懶了。（slack off）

_____

8. 凡事得來不易。（come）

_____

9. 我真希望自己能長得高一點。（wish）

_____

10. 你最近在迷什麼？（into）

_____

解答 1

1) I don't buy your story.　2) Why the long face?　3) I'm sorry to hear that.　4) I broke up with my boyfriend.　5) I suck at cooking.　6) I'm craving meat.　7) I shouldn't have slacked off. 8) Nothing comes easy.　9) I wish I were taller.　10) What are you into these days?

依照句意填入正確答案。

1. 醒醒吧。

Wake up and smell _____.

2. 別人碗裡的東西看起來特別好吃。

Grass is always greener _____.

3. 沉穩踏實者終將得勝。

_____ wins the race.

4. 事出必有因。

Everything happens _____.

5. 我垂涎欲滴。

My mouth _____.

6. 我們去吃點小東西吧。

Let's go grab_____.

7. 覆水難收。

It's no use crying _____.

8. 事情已成定局。

What's done _____.

9. 江山易改，本性難移。

A leopard _____ its spots.

10. 有志者事竟成。

Where _____ there is a way.

解答 2

1) the coffee   2) on the other side   3) Slow and steady   4) for a reason   5) is watering
6) a bite   7) over spilt milk   8) is done   9) can't change   10) there is a will

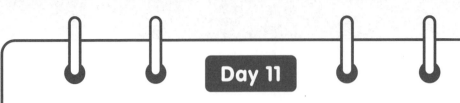

Pain in the ass
讓人恨得牙癢癢的大麻煩

應該不難察覺到，美國人經常在罵人的話中用到「屁股」這個字。屁股的英文原本是 buttocks，口語上大部分稱為 butt，ass 則是比較粗俗的說法。有 asshole（混蛋）；buttface（醜八怪／蠢蛋）；kiss my ass.（別做夢了）；I'll kick your ass.（我會打爆你）；LMAO: Laughing my ass off.（笑死）；bust my ass（賣命工作）；dumbass（蠢貨）等衍生用法。要了解 butt 和 ass 在語感上的細微差異，才可以完全體會兩者語氣的強弱。如果 pain in the butt 是「煩人的討厭鬼」，那 pain in the ass 就更粗俗一點，可以理解為「煩死人的討厭鬼」。

John	Damn it! My laptop won't start again!
Kamila	What? Didn't you get it fixed last week?
John	Uh, huh. This is a real 💬 **pain in the ass**. It's really pissing me off.
Kamila	I think it's time to get a new one.
John	It's gonna cost an arm and a leg. I'm so broke these days. Gosh!

約翰	該死！我的筆電又打不開了！
卡蜜拉	什麼？你上禮拜不是拿去修了嗎？
約翰	對啊，這台筆電真的是在找我麻煩，快讓我氣死了。
卡蜜拉	或許該換一台新的了。
約翰	那我要先去賣腎才行，我最近在吃土，唉！

TAIGLISH 別再說「notebook」了！

notebook 是「超小型筆電」，甚至外國人直接想到的是「筆記本」！實際上我們一般用的 13 吋筆電稱為 laptop，也就是可放在 lap（大腿）上用的電腦，而放在 desk（書桌）上用的桌上型電腦則稱為 desktop。

EXPRESSION 「開機」、「發動車子」用英文怎麼說？

跟本文一樣用 start 就可以了。「發動車子」就是 start the car。

SLANG piss someone off

查字典的話會出現「讓人很生氣」的結果，但這個解釋其實無法確切表現出原文的語感。Piss someone off 可以說是「讓人很火大」，或是更口語化地用「讓人一肚子火」來表示。

IDIOM cost an arm and leg

直譯為「剁手剁腳來付」，相當於中文「賣腎才付得起」，表示「燒錢、十分昂貴」。

This car cost me an arm and a leg.
這台車讓我噴了超多錢。

EXPRESSION I'm so broke.

我斷掉了？ No! broke 當作形容詞使用時，是「破產」的意思。母語者常用這句話表示沒錢。

I'm so broke this month. I don't even have 5 dollars.
我這個月窮到脫褲，連 5 塊錢都沒有。

Beauty is only skin deep
內在美更重要

skin deep 意味著「膚淺的」，這句話是在説「美貌只是表面的」，比起看得見的外在美，看不見的人品、個性更重要。為自己的外貌投資之餘，也要記得花時間累積內涵，培養出可以欣賞他人靈魂之美的眼光！

Whitney What kind of girls do you go for?

Billy I used to only go for pretty girls but I've realized that 💬 **beauty is only skin deep**.

Whitney I couldn't agree more but girls always go for jocks too!

Billy One day, they will all realize that looks aren't everything.

Whitney Dang! This is deep, bro.

惠妮 你喜歡什麼樣的女生？

比利 我以前只喜歡正妹，但我現在已經懂了，美貌只是表面的。

惠妮 我超同意這一點，可是女生也只對學校那些體育男有興趣！

比利 她們總有一天也會明白外貌不代表一切。

惠妮 哇！這句話很深奧耶，哥。

EXPRESSION **go for**

go for 有五種不同意思：

1. 喜歡、偏愛
I go for sweet guys.
我喜歡溫柔親切的男生。

2. 撲向、襲擊
The dog went for its neighbor.
那隻狗襲擊了鄰居。

3. 選擇
I'm gonna go for a Vanilla latte.
我要一杯香草拿鐵。

4. 採取行動；爭取
Go for it!
去做吧；加油！

5. 適用於
The rule goes for you, too.
這個規定也適用於你身上。

EXPRESSION **I couldn't agree more.**

不能再同意更多，同意程度已經高達極限，就是完全同意。I can't agree more. 是比較直接的說法，而 I couldn't agree more. 用假設語氣，語氣較委婉。雖然兩者都沒有文法上的錯誤，不過對母語者來說 I couldn't 聽起來會比 I can't 自然。類似的用法還有 I couldn't be happier.（我開心得不得了。）或 It couldn't be worse.（情況不能再糟了。）等。

CULTURE **jocks**

jock 泛指「（高中或大學的）運動選手」。美國高中的美式足球選手稱作 jocks，一般給人長相帥氣、好身材的人氣男神印象。美國高校電影中經常出現 jocks 這種小鮮肉，女朋友通常是漂亮又受歡迎的啦啦隊隊員。

Jocks usually win Prom king. 長得帥的美式足球選手獲選為舞會國王是常有的事。
*prom 是美國高中舞會，11 年級跟 12 年級生可參加，並選出年度舞會國王、王后。

SLANG **Dang!**

dang 是 damn 的委婉說法，當感嘆詞使用，用來表達「哇，天啊！」、「讚！」、「嗚哇！」等吃驚反應。

Dang! She's hot! 哇，天啊！她好辣！

SLANG **bro**

bro 是 brother 的簡稱，也可以用 bro 稱呼男性好友。

We've been bros since ten. 我們從 10 歲起就是好兄弟。

Everything fell into place
一切都順利進行 / 一切都合理說得通

事情完美到位,達到所有條件,獲得滿意結果。也就是我們常說的「天時、地利、人和」。

Don't say once everything falls into place you will find peace.
Find your peace then everything will fall into place.

別說只有一切順利解決,內心才能得到平靜。
只要你內心平靜下來,事情就會迎刃而解。

Reporter	What is your secret to such great success?
Author	Consistency, never giving up and believing in myself.
Reporter	Do you think luck also played an important role in your success?
Author	Absolutely! 💬 **Everything just fell into place.**
Reporter	Now things are falling into place for me.
Author	However, success comes to only those who are ready for it.

記者	請問妳的成功秘訣是什麼呢?
作者	堅持、不放棄、相信自己。
記者	妳認為自己的成功有運氣的成分嗎?
作者	當然!這要歸功於天時、地利、人和。
記者	對我來說,也漸漸拼湊出故事的全貌了。
作者	不過,成功是留給準備好的人的。

EXPRESSION **play an important role**

戲劇中的角色稱為 role，在某件事中扮演重要角色，指「起了重要作用」，表示影響重大的因素。

Trust plays a crucial role in maintaining a good relationship.
信任是維繫一段良好關係的關鍵。

EXPRESSION **Absolutely ！**

想要表示「當然！」，只會說 of course! 嗎？下次試著用母語者常說的 absolutely!，應用於各種情況強調「完全沒錯」，是電影或美劇中經常使用到的表達方式。

You are absolutely right.
你說的完全沒錯。

Yes, I absolutely want whipped cream on top.
對，我上面絕對要加鮮奶油。

IDIOM **Now things are falling into place for me.**

本文中第二次出現這句慣用語時，並不是「天時、地利、人和」的意思，而是表示「現在一切都說得通了」，也就是「我了解作家為何成功了」。要記得這句話也有「我懂了」的意思！

Oh! The bits of the puzzle are finally falling into place!
哦！終於拼上最後一塊拼圖了！

Everything fell into place after finding out the truth.
查清事實後，一切都明朗了。

PROVERB **Success comes to only those who are ready for it.**

「成功是留給做好準備的人」的意思。類似的說法還有 Success only comes to those who dare to attempt.「成功是屬於勇於嘗試的人」。

Karma is a bitch
惡有惡報

業障（karma）指過去的善舉或惡行，未來都會帶來業報，也就是「種什麼因，得什麼果」、「因果報應」。用字典查 bitch，會出現「母狗」的意思，髒話則意味「婊子」，也可表達令人不爽的狀況或人物。通常被用於指稱女性，不過偶爾也會用在男性身上。例如 Life is a bitch.（人生好難）、It hurts like a bitch!（痛死我了）。有時好友之間也會開玩笑地互稱 bitch，類似「小賤貨」的暱稱。例如 Hi, pretty bitches!（嗨，各位漂亮小婊子）bitch 在俚語中可變化為 biotch 。What's up, biotch!（怎麼啦？小賤貨們！）

Sarah　　I can't believe Jenny stabbed me in the back.
Liam　　I know it hurts but let it go.
Sarah　　I wasn't able to sleep at all last night.
Liam　　Trust me. 💬 **Karma is a bitch**. What goes around comes around.
Sarah　　I really hope so.

莎拉　　我真的無法相信，珍妮竟然背叛我。
連恩　　我知道妳很傷心，但妳得學會放下。
莎拉　　我昨晚完全沒睡。
連恩　　相信我，報應是很可怕的，惡有惡報，善有善報。
莎拉　　如果真的是這樣就好了。

stab (someone) in the back

「在某人背後捅刀」，也就是「背叛」的意思。

I got stabbed in the back by someone I trust.
我被信任的人在背後捅刀。

Never stab me in the back.
絕對不要背叛我。

 Let it go.

迪士尼動畫電影《冰雪奇緣》原聲帶，最受全球觀眾喜愛的歌曲〈Let It Go〉，意思是拋開令人心煩的一切；忘掉後悔的過去；放下難以忘懷的舊愛。

Let it be.（「披頭四」歌曲）
順其自然。

Let it flow.
任其流動。

Let her be.
讓她做自己。/ 隨她去吧。

Let him go now.
放下他吧。

MOSR MISTAKEN **last night**

「昨晚」直譯成 yesterday night 是大家時常犯的錯誤之一，實際上不存在這種用法，正確說法是 last night。類似的錯誤還有 today morning，要說 this morning 才對。

yesterday night (X) ▶ last night (O)
today morning (X) ▶ this morning (O)

I slept early last night.
我昨晚比較早睡。

I had a huge breakfast this morning.
我今天早上吃了一頓豐盛的早餐。

PROVERB **What goes around comes around.**

如同字面上的意思，「如何對待別人，終究會回報到自己身上」。此外，類似表達還有 You get what you give.（一分耕耘一分收穫）；You reap what you sow.（種什麼因得什麼果）。

Say nice things and perform good deeds.
What goes around comes around.
說好話，做好事。種善因，得善果。

Life happens
人生不如意十有八九

人生在世，有時事情會因為各種意料之外的大小變化無法按計畫進行，也難免有突然遭逢意外或失業、經濟困難或失去摯友的時刻。有時也會碰上丟失錢包、打翻咖啡、穿不下最喜歡的衣服等令人沮喪的小事。以上情形都可說 Life happens.，這是 Shit happens.（走在路上難免踩到狗屎）的委婉說法。

Cathy	Excuse me. Are you John by any chance?
John	Cathy?
Cathy	Oh my God! It's been ages! I thought you went to the States to study.
John	My grand plans are shelved. 💬 **Life happens**, you know?
Cathy	Do you have some time to catch up? Dinner's on me!

凱西	不好意思，你該不會是約翰吧？
約翰	凱西？
凱西	天啊！幾百年沒見到你了！我以為你去美國念書了。
約翰	我的遠大計畫停擺了。人生不如意十有八九，妳說是吧？
凱西	你有空嗎？跟我聊聊，更新一下近況吧。晚餐我請！

EXPRESSION **by any chance**

表示「也許」或「詢問可能性」，特別常用於疑問句。

Do you have a pen, by any chance?
你有筆嗎？

Have we met before, by any chance?
我們之前見過面嗎？

EXPRESSION **It's been ages!**

ages 類似於 years，但語氣上給人時間更長的感覺。就像中文「八百年沒見了」一樣，表示時間過了很久。類似的表達還有 It's been a while. / It's been a long time. / Long time no see. 等。此外，gazillion 代表數也數不清的天文數字，所以也有人用 It's been gazillion years! 表現更誇張的語氣。（浮誇是美國人的講話特色）

EXPRESSION **catch up**

趕上前人腳步，或跟上課程進度。也可以像本文一樣，用 catch up 表示很久沒聊天的朋友，敘舊更新彼此近況。

I have a lot to catch up in class.
我還有很多課程進度沒跟上。

Go first. I'll catch up with you in a min!
你先走，我隨後跟上！

MOSR MISTAKEN **on me 不是在我身上！**

It's on me. 意思是「交給我來負責」，表示「我付帳」、「這餐我請」。請客類似的說法還有 I'll treat you out. / It's my treat. 等。

It's on me this time!
這次我請！

Coffee is on me since you treated me to lunch.
既然你請我吃午餐，咖啡就讓我請吧。

Been there done that
我也是過來人 / 早已見識過

原本完整的句子是 I've been there and done that.，不過一般口語會省略主詞。意思是曾經置身某種情況，經歷過某事。此句有兩種用法，一表示共鳴，告訴對方自己也有相同經歷；二是自己早就經歷過了，這種事沒什麼大不了的。因此想表示不願意再繼續做某事，或不想重蹈覆轍的時候，也可以說這句話。但是要小心，說這種話的時候可能會令人覺得在倚老賣老。

Mom   Did you smoke? You smell like cigarettes.

Son   No...

Mom   💬 **Been there done that.** I used to smoke back in high school due to peer pressure.

Son   Really? But I'm afraid that I might get bullied if I don't.

Mom   I know it's hard to resist peer pressure but don't lose yourself. Man up and say No!

媽媽   你是不是抽菸？身上有菸味。

兒子   沒有啊……

媽媽   我也年輕過。我高中時因為同儕壓力抽過菸。

兒子   真假？但我怕不抽會被霸凌。

媽媽   我懂，同儕壓力很難反抗，但不要迷失自我。硬起來說不！

MOST CONFUSED I used to vs. I am used to

台灣人很容易搞混的句型，儘管看起來相似，但意思卻截然不同。本文中出現的「I used to + 原形動詞」是「我以前經常～」，表示以前曾做過某事，但現在已經不再做了；「I am used to + 名詞 / 動名詞」則是「現在習慣（某事物）～」。別再搞混囉！

✦ **I used to +** 原形動詞
我以前經常～

I used to live in Seoul.
我以前住在首爾。

She used to drink green tea.
她以前常喝綠茶。

✦ **I'm used to +** 名詞 / 動名詞
我習慣～

I'm used to living in Seoul.
我習慣住在首爾的生活。

She is used to drinking green tea.
她習慣喝綠茶。

EXPRESSION peer pressure

來自同僚、朋友等團體的壓力，尤其常見於青少年之間。這種壓力使少數群體傾向默默跟從多數群體的意見，多數情況下帶有貶義。但有時朋友努力，你也跟著努力，就有正面意義。

I won't let peer pressure change my values.
我不會任憑同儕壓力影響改變我的價值觀。

EXPRESSION 「霸凌」用英文怎麼說？

bully 是排擠、嘲弄、施暴、人身攻擊，以及脅迫他人等各種行為的統稱。當名詞使用時，則是指稱行使這些行為的霸凌者，或者可以翻譯成「惡霸」。

He bullied her into stealing money.
他強迫她偷錢。

Cyber bullying is a serious issue these days.
網路霸凌近年來已構成嚴重問題。

IDIOM Man up!

激勵對方「像個男子漢一樣」，勇往直前做某事，或負起男人擔當的責任。類似說法還有 Toughen up!；Be a man about it. 等。

Stop crying and man up!
別哭了，拿出男子氣概來！

Keep calm and carry on
保持冷靜，繼續前進

這句話是二戰期間，英國政府為了鼓舞民心，製作的宣傳海報標語，寓意是無論身處於什麼情況，都要冷靜自持，繼續向前邁進。這句話衍生出無數的翻玩作品，時至今日仍受到全世界的喜愛，印著這句話的馬克杯、衣服、地毯、筆及紀念品等在英國隨處可見。也可以改成各種動詞，例如 Keep calm and eat a cake.（保持冷靜，吃塊蛋糕）；Keep calm and dream big.（保持冷靜，胸懷大志）；Keep calm and listen to music.（保持冷靜，聽聽音樂）等。

Daughter I try so hard but my business isn't taking off.

Dad Rome was not built in a day. Just 💬 **keep calm and carry on**.

Daughter That's so true.

Dad Overnight success is a myth.

Daughter Thanks, Daddy. I should get myself together.

女兒 我已經很努力了，但我的事業還是停滯不前。

爸爸 羅馬不是一天造成的。保持冷靜，繼續前進吧。

女兒 你說得對。

爸爸 想一夕成功是不可能的。

女兒 謝啦，爸。我會振作起來的。

EXPRESSION 「爆紅」用英文要怎麼說？

take off 有「起飛；離開；脫掉」等涵義。在本文裡是當作「事業起飛」、「受歡迎」，也就是「竄紅」的意思。

My flight is taking off soon.（起飛）
我的班機即將起飛。

Take off your coat.（脫掉）
脫掉你的大衣。

Did you take off?（離開）
你離開了嗎？

My career started taking off last year.（開始成功）
我的事業從去年開始有了起色。

PROVERB Rome was not built in a day.

羅馬不是一天造成的，從繁榮盛世的帝國首都，到現代義大利首都，經過了數千年歲月的淬鍊。任何事都不可能一蹴而就，提醒世人按部就班勿躁進。

EXPRESSION overnight success

意指一夕成名，毫不費力就突然大獲成功。

Overnight success actually takes many years.
一夕成功的背後其實有著多年的努力。

There is no such thing as overnight success.
沒有一夕成功這種事。

IDIOM get oneself together

把散亂的思緒和想法集中起來，打起精神。類似的說法還有 pull oneself together，有平復心情，保持平靜的涵義。

She quit drinking and got herself together.
她把酒戒掉，振作了起來。

I took a deep breath and pulled myself together.
我深呼吸，讓自己平靜下來。

Netflix and chill
看 Netflix 耍廢

語言會反映時代的變遷，最近在美國看 Netflix 的人似乎比看電視的人還要多，因而也出現了把 Netflix 當作動詞使用的用法，就像 Google it!（估狗搜尋）；Instagram my brunch（哀居上傳網美早午餐）一樣，也可以說 I Netflixed last night.（我昨晚看了 Netflix），也可以加上 chill，說 I Netflix and chilled last night.（我昨晚在看 Netflix 耍廢）不過要注意，Netflix and chill 也有類似「我家今晚沒人」的性暗示含義，要看上下文小心使用。

Bob　　What did you do over the weekend?

Lora　　I was just home this whole weekend.

Bob　　What in the world did you do all alone?

Lora　　I was a total couch potato. Just 💬 **Netflix and chilled**.

Bob　　You really love vegging out, huh?

鮑伯　　妳週末在幹嘛？

蘿拉　　我整個週末都待在家。

鮑伯　　妳一個人到底都在做什麼？

蘿拉　　我整天癱在沙發上看 Netflix。

鮑伯　　妳真的很愛耍廢耶？

MOST CONFUSED — over vs. during

「你週末在做什麼？」常被直譯為 What did you do during the weekend? 這句話雖然沒有文法上的錯誤，不過母語者更常用 over the weekend。during 指週末期間的某個時間點；over 類似 throughout，表達一整個週末的意思（週五到週日）。

over	during
I studied English over the weekend.	**I studied English during the weekend.**
我整個週末都在讀英文。	我週末有讀英文。
	＊週末期間有讀英文，也有做別的事
I went to Paris over summer vacation.	**I went to Paris during summer vacation.**
我整個暑假都在巴黎。	我暑假去了一趟巴黎。
	＊暑假很長，並非兩個月都在巴黎

EXPRESSION — What in the world ~?

「天啊，到底是怎麼回事？」的意思。後面加上子句，強調難以理解某事的錯愕感。前面也可以改成 when、where、what、how、why 等疑問詞，類似的慣用語 What on earth ~? / What the hell ~? 等。

What in the world are you talking about?
你到底在說什麼？

Where in the world are you?
你到底在哪裡？

When in the world are you going to clean your room?
你到底什麼時候才要打掃房間？

How in the world did you do that?
你到底是怎麼做到的？

IDIOM — couch potato

躺著追劇耍廢，這個大家都知道，但為什麼用「馬鈴薯」形容？美國人追劇時，非常愛配超大包的洋芋片，一手拿洋芋片，一手拿啤酒，整個人攤在沙發上，所以才有這個「沙發馬鈴薯」的慣用語。

SPOKEN ENGLISH — veg out

「什麼都不做，放鬆耍廢」的意思。看到 veg 這個字，是不是聯想到 veggie 了呢？veggie 是 vegetable 的簡稱，所以 veg out 這句動詞片語就是在形容人像植物一樣待在原地一動也不動。

I only vegged out over the weekend.
我整個週末都在耍廢。

Monday blues
週一症候群

在美國，「藍色」象徵憂鬱。如果你看過迪士尼動畫《腦筋急轉彎》（Inside Out），裡頭象徵憂鬱的角色也是藍色的。I feel blue. 即「我很憂鬱」，Monday blues 就是我們常說的「週一症候群」，此外也有 Sunday blues，意為星期一即將來臨，突然想到要上班就感到憂鬱。

Linda   I hate 💬 **Monday blues**. I wish I didn't have to work.

Ben   You need to take the glass half full approach. I'm thankful that I can pay my rent.

Linda   I need a coffee with an extra shot.

Ben   I'll buy you coffee. Feel better.

Linda   You are absolutely my go-to guy!

琳達   我討厭週一症候群，好希望不用去上班。

班   往好的方向想，我很感謝工作讓我付得起房租。

琳達   我需要一杯咖啡加一份濃縮。

班   我請妳，加油。

琳達   你最棒了！

EXPRESSION Take the glass half full approach

Is the glass half empty or half full?（杯子空了一半；或是還有半杯水？）這個問題讓人領悟到，任何事都取決於自己的觀點。看著一樣的水，有的人會因為杯子還有半杯水而開心，有的人則會因為杯子少了半杯水而難過，因此 Take the glass half full approach. 告訴我們「正面思考」的寓意。

EXPRESSION 「不要加……」用英文怎麼說？

美國人喜歡照自己的口味選擇要吃什麼，典型的例子有「星巴克」和「Subway」。在咖啡廳或餐廳點餐時，使用 with 和 without。請店家添加東西時，也可以用 add。

不要加～	幫我加～
Can I have it without cilantro? 可以不要加香菜嗎？	**Can I have it with extra Caramel drizzle on top?** 上面可以幫我多淋點焦糖嗎？
Can I have my burger without pickles? 我的漢堡可以不要加酸黃瓜嗎？	**Can you add Vanilla syrup to my coffee?** 我的咖啡可以幫加香草糖漿嗎？

MOST CONFUSED rent vs. lease

rent 和 lease 都是「租借」的意思，rent 通常指的是一個月以下的短期租借；lease 的租期大約為一年。房租因為是月繳，所以用 rent，對話中使用名詞，當「租金」。car rental 是為了旅行而短租車子的服務；car lease 則可以租借幾年。很多美國人喜歡租長期的車子勝過買車，他們也很常長租冰箱、洗衣機等家電用品。

Hi, I would like to rent a car for 2 days.
您好，我想租兩天的車。

SLANG go-to

go-to 指在特定情況下必須或最佳的人選（person）或事物（something）。為了取得資訊、建議或協助而「去（go-to）」，也就是「必找／必去的人事物」。

This is my go-to café when I want a cheap and quick coffee.
這間咖啡廳是當我想來杯便宜又快速的咖啡必來的地方。

It's a go-to place for Instagram.
這裡是很適合拍照上傳 IG 的地方。

Reveal one's true colors
露出本性

reveal 意為「顯露」，不過多為負面的用法，揭發不為人知的本性、秘辛等。顯露出一個人真實的顏色，也就是「露出本性」的意思。

Mary   I just wanted to say, 'Thank you'. I really appreciate your presence.

Lucas   What? What has gotten into you?

Mary   People I used to call friends 💬 **revealed their true colors** when I was having the worst time of my life. But you've always been there for me.

Lucas   Don't even go there. That's what friends are for.

瑪麗   我只是想跟你說聲「謝謝」，我真的很感謝有你在。

路卡斯   什麼？妳吃錯藥嗎？

瑪麗   在我人生最低潮的時候，那些被我當作朋友的人都一個個露出本性，但是你卻一直在我身邊。

路卡斯   別客氣，朋友當假的哦。

EXPRESSION I appreciate it.

母語者很常説 I appreciate it.，甚至會和 Thank you. 連用。這個用法比 Thank you. 更誠懇，也很體面。appreciate 還有「賞識、欣賞」等意思。學到了吧？趁機甩掉用到爛的 Thank you. 吧。

I appreciate your love and support.
感謝你的愛與支持。

I would appreciate it if you can come at 7.
如果你能七點來，我會很感謝。

EXPRESSION What has gotten into you?

直譯是「有什麼東西跑進你體內」，即「你被附身了嗎？怎麼了？」的意思。當對方表現得不一樣，行為詭異的時候，就可以使用。got / gotten 皆正確。

What's gotten into you? This isn't you!
你怎麼了？這一點也不像你！

EXPRESSION You've (always) been there for me.

直譯為「為了我，你總是在那裡」。意為無論我現在處境低潮或順遂，你總在我身邊。當你難過時，就可以對身邊依然支持你的朋友、家人説這句。

Alison has been there for me when I was going through hardships.
艾莉森在我低潮時總是在我身邊。

You know I'm here for you, right?
你知道我一直都在，對吧？

＊當主詞是第一人稱時，使用 here 比 there 自然。

EXPRESSION Don't (even) go there.

不要去那裡？ No! 這句話的意思是「不要再講下去了」，類似 Don't mention it.，小事一樁，不需道謝的意思。此外，當不想再繼續某話題，或因為話題敏感，可能會傷到某人，在對方越線之前，也可説這句提出警告。

Don't go there. I don't want to talk about it right now.
夠了，我現在不想説那件事。

Let's Practice!
DAY 11-20

Exercise 1 請用題目中給的單字造句。

1. 這真的好煩！（pain）

_____

2. 珍妮背叛了我！（stab）

_____

3. 我請客！（on）

_____

4. 保持平常心，持續前進。（Keep calm）

_____

5. 振作！（put）

_____

6. 真的好久不見！（ages）

_____

7. 像個男子漢！（man）

_____

8. 我在家耍廢。（veg）

_____

9. 一切都水到渠成。（fall into）

_____

10. 你喜歡什麼樣的男人？（go for）

_____

解答 1

1) This is pain in the ass!   2) Jenny stabbed me in the back!   3) It's on me!   4) Keep calm and carry on.   5) Put yourself together!   6) It's been ages!   7) Man up!   8) I vegged out at home. 9) Everything fell into place.   10) What kind of guy do you go for?

1. 我最近沒錢。

I'm _____ these days.

2. 報應是很可怕的。

_____ is a _____.

3. 要不要一起看 Netflix 耍廢？

Do you wanna _____?

4. 他露出他的本色。

He _____ his _____.

5. 你吃錯藥哦？

What has _____?

6. 我是過來人。

_____and done that.

7. 內在美更重要。

_____ is only skin deep.

8. 我討厭週一症候群。

I hate _____.

9. 羅馬不是一天造成的。

_____ built in _____.

10. 人生不會照著計畫進行。

_____ happens.

解答 2
1) broke 2) Karma, bitch 3) Netflix and chill 4) revealed, true colors 5) gotten into you
6) Been there 7) Beauty 8) Monday blues 9) Rome was not, a day 10) Life

You've got to crack a few eggs to make an omelet

你想有所得，就勢必得有所犧牲

字面上的意思「想煎歐姆蛋捲，就得打破雞蛋」，也就是為了達成目標或獲得成果，就必須付出代價或有所犧牲。想獲得就得甘心付出代價，不是嗎？

Matt	I want to start my own business but I'm too scared to quit my stable job.
Lora	Well, you've got to crack a few eggs to make an omelet.
Matt	I didn't think of that.
Lora	It's OK to fail or make mistakes. But if you fall down seven times, you must stand up eight.
Matt	Alright! I'll take my chances.

麥特	我想開創我的事業，但是我害怕辭掉穩定的工作。
蘿拉	嗯，你想有所得，就必有所失。
麥特	我倒是沒想到這點。
蘿拉	就算失敗或失誤也沒關係，但是你得七轉八起。
麥特	沒錯！我要賭一把。

MOST MISTAKEN scared vs. scary

很多人會將「我害怕」說錯成 I'm scary.，但 scary 是「令人害怕的」，變成「我是可怕的人物」。如果想表達感到害怕，在英文是「被使感到害怕的」，用過去分詞 p.p. 構成被動語態 I'm scared.；現在分詞 -ing 則表達主動「令人感到……的」。讓我們來看看經常犯錯的經典例子吧。

p.p. 過去分詞	-ing 現在分詞
I'm bored. 我覺得無聊。	**I'm boring.** 我是令人無聊的人。
I'm interested. 我有興趣。	**I'm interesting.** 我這個人很有趣。
excited reporters 興奮的記者們	**exciting news** 讓人興奮的新聞
confused students 感到困惑的學生們	**confusing questions** 讓人困惑的問題
tired students 疲倦的學生們	**tiring job** 讓人感到疲倦的工作

MOST MISTAKEN quit vs. stop

quit 大部分指「徹底停止」長期責任、習慣；stop 則是指「暫時停止動作」。例如 I quit my job. 是辭職的意思，但 I stopped working. 是暫時停止工作。只要不是辭去工作或從學校退學，stop 比 quit 更常使用。stop 後面若接不定詞 to V，則是代表「暫停目前動作，改去做～」。

quit	stop
I quit smoking. 我戒菸了。	**I stopped smoking.** [stop + 動詞 -ing] 我戒菸了。／我暫時停止抽菸。 **vs.** **I stopped to smoke.** [stop + to 不定詞] 我停下手邊的事，去抽菸。

PROVERB Fall down seven times, stand up eight.

字面上的意思是「跌倒七次，站起來八次」，日文也有相似的成語「七轉八起」，即「人生不如意十之八九」，即使不斷失敗，也要重新站起來挑戰。

IDIOM I'll take my chances.

意為「賭賭看」，也就是即使有風險，也要冒險一試的意思。

Don't take your chances if you don't have a plan B.
如果你沒有替代方案，就不要冒險。

Beauty is in the eye of the beholder

情人眼裡出西施

古希臘哲學家柏拉圖的名言。此處 beholder 指的是「觀看者」或「旁觀者」，所以這句話的寓意就是「美的定義依觀看者的喜好和標準有所不同」。

Sarah   Have you seen Jenny's boyfriend?

Luke   No, why?

Sarah   I don't know why she is going out with him. They don't look good together at all.

Luke   Why? Because of how they dress and look? 💬 **Beauty lies in the eye of the beholder.** Beauty comes in every shape and form. He must be a wonderful guy, for Jenny to date him.

莎拉   你有看到珍妮的男友嗎？

盧克   沒有。怎麼了？

莎拉   我不懂她為什麼跟那個人交往，他們兩個看起來很不配。

盧克   為什麼？因為他們的風格跟外表嗎？情人眼裡出西施，美有各種形態跟形式。既然珍妮選擇了他，就代表他一定是個很棒的人。

EXPRESSION **go out**

go out 表示「出去」，不過也有「交往」的意思。如果有人問 Would you go out with me?，不是「要跟我出去嗎？」，而是問「要跟我交往嗎？」。也可以在 go out 後面用介系詞 with 加上交往對象。

I'm going out with Jay.
我在跟杰交往。

We've been going out for 4 years.
我們已經交往四年了。

EXPRESSION **「很配」用英文怎麼說？**

「情侶很相配」常常被直譯為 They match well.，這樣的說法不太通順。想要自然地表達相配的意思，可以使用本文中的 look good together，還有 well matched；a match made in heaven；so meant to be together；well suited to each other 等用法。

GRAMMAR **must**

「必須」的助動詞。用法與 have to 相似，不過語氣更強烈。另外，也可以用來表達「一定是～」，表示肯定程度高的推測，當作推測的意思使用時，容易與 should、may、might 混淆，就趁這個機會搞清楚其中的差異吧。

musts > should > may > might

Lora must be home now.
蘿拉一定在家。
* 我 100% 肯定！

Lora should be home now.
蘿拉應該在家。
* 無法完全確定，80%

Lora may be home now.
蘿拉大概在家。
* 我覺得是這樣，60%

Lora might be home now.
蘿拉可能在家，也可能不在。
* 也有這個可能性，50%

GRAMMAR **可以把 for 當作連接詞使用？**

Yes! 一直都以為 for 只能當作介系詞使用，解釋成「為了～」的話，那麼下方的句子就說不通了。for 也可以當作連接詞，用法類似 because。使用 because 時，原因和結果明確，句意偏重在結果，而使用 for 時，前後兩個子句重要性對等。

Jenny was crying, for she broke up with her boyfriend.
珍妮因為跟男友分手了在哭。

She studied English, for she wanted to travel all around the world.
她學英文是想要環遊世界。

Get it out of one's system
抒發心情

system 最廣為人知的詞義是「系統」，不過也代表「身體」，所以這句話有「把負面情緒（尤其是憤怒）宣洩到體外」的意思，就像做瑜伽時經由呼吸排空思緒和情緒一樣。也表示達成長期以來渴望、盼望的事物，不再執迷不捨的心態。此外，也有字面上的「把物質排出體內」的意思。

Jen	I'm still so angry and I don't know what to do!
Dave	Why don't we take a walk to 💬 **get it out of your system**?
Jen	Would that help?
Dave	Let's give it a shot. We have plenty of time! It can't hurt.
Jen	Thanks for listening to me vent.

簡	我還是很不爽，不知道要怎麼做才好！
戴夫	我們散個步，抒發一下心情吧？
簡	有用嗎？
戴夫	試試看嘛，反正我們時間多得是！不會有什麼壞處。
簡	謝謝你聽我抱怨。

GRAMMAR 溫和委婉的 would ！

would 有很多種用法，我們來認識一下本文中的用法吧。如果 will 是單刀直入的辣味，那 would 就是比較溫和的口味。舉例來說，I will do it. 是「我會做」，語感上傳達出一定會做的強烈意志；I would do it. 則比較接近「我有打算要做」。而 would 的語氣比起 will 較不直接，所以聽起來更有禮貌。兩者在語意上沒有太大差別，但是有細微的語感差異。

It will help.
會有幫助。

It would help.
應該有幫助。

Will you marry me?
你要跟我結婚嗎？

Would you marry me?
你願意跟我結婚嗎？

Will you help me?
你要不要幫我？

Would you help me?
你可以幫我嗎？

IDIOM Give it a shot.

意思是「嘗試一次看看」，同樣的表達方式還有 Give it a try. 或是 Give it a go.。用來表示「提起勇氣嘗試沒做過的事情」。

I have never tried stinky tofu but I'll give it a shot.
我沒吃過臭豆腐，不過我會試試看。

Ask her out. Just give it a shot!
約她出來看看，衝了啦。

EXPRESSION It can't hurt.

那又不會痛？這句話中的痛可以解釋為「傷害」。也就是做「某事也不會有害」；「反正也不吃虧」；「又不會少一塊肉」；「又不會怎樣？」的意思。也可以變化為 It wouldn't hurt. 或是 It doesn't hurt. 等做使用。

It wouldn't hurt to apologize first.
先低頭道歉又不會少一塊肉。

EXPRESSION vent

宣洩內心的負面情緒。vent 是「通風口」，用「釋放情緒的通風口」去想的話就很好理解。指的是被壓力搞得心情鬱悶，或氣到怒髮衝冠時，和朋友聊聊傾訴、吶喊、大哭當作宣洩，或是向某人抱怨、發火的意思。

I shouldn't have vented my anger on you.
我不該把我的憤怒發洩在你身上。

Learn how to vent your negative emotions in a peaceful manner.
學習以平緩的方式排解負面情緒。

Blowing out of proportion
小題大作

常聽到台灣人説「太 over」，這是台式英文！正確的表達方式有 <u>go overboard</u>；<u>overreact</u>；<u>extra</u> 等，而 <u>blowing (something) out of proportion</u> 也是母語使用者常用的説法，「不符比例的膨脹」，也就是「過於誇張、小題大作」的意思。

David   I think Linette likes me.

Lora   Where is this coming from?

David   She gave me a chocolate for helping her with her homework.

Lora   That's it? You are 💬 **blowing this out of proportion**. You are totally misunderstanding her nice gesture. Wake up, David.

David   Ouch! A dagger to the heart!

大衛   我覺得蕾妮特喜歡我。

蘿拉   為什麼你會這樣覺得？

大衛   我幫忙她的作業，她就給我巧克力。

蘿拉   就這樣？你過度反應了吧，誤會她的好意了。
醒醒吧，大衛。

大衛   噢！不要這樣打擊我！

EXPRESSION **Where is this coming from?**

直譯是「這是哪來的？」，不過可以解釋為「你為什麼這麼說？」、「為什麼突然這麼想？」、「說什麼蠢話？」、「這麼做的原因是什麼？」。比方說某人突然發脾氣的時候，就可以用這句話詢問對方為什麼這麼生氣，憤怒的根源從何而來。

I don't understand where this is coming from!
我完全不懂為什麼會這樣；我完全不懂他為什麼這麼說！

You need to know where I'm coming from.
你要知道我為什麼會這樣。

MOST MISTAKEN **That's it. vs. I'm finished.**

有些人結束自我介紹時會用 finish 來作結，I'm finished. 有「做完某事、完成某事」或是「收尾」的意思，用在這種情況下其實有點生硬，比較自然的說法是 That's it.，代表「就這樣」；「就到這裡」。下次在餐廳點完餐時，就用 That's it. 來表示結束吧。而全部吃完，請服務生收盤子的時候，則可以用 I'm finished.。此外，That's it! 還可以用來表示「就是這個！」或「夠了！」的意思。

Can I have a latte and a hot chocolate? That's it.
我想要一杯拿鐵、一杯熱巧克力。這樣就好。

That's it! I'm gonna say something!
夠了！我一定要說些什麼才行！

EXPRESSION **nice gesture**

gesture 意味著「姿勢、手勢」，不過也用來表示「有禮的行動」、「善舉」或是「好意」，例如 nice gesture；sweet gesture；kind gesture。

Saying 'Thank you' is always a kind gesture.
把「謝謝」掛嘴邊總是不會失禮。

IDIOM **A dagger to the heart!**

把刀插在心上！這句話可以當作感嘆詞使用，有人說話直接得像在自己心上捅刀的時候，就這樣回答對方吧。也可以像本文一樣用開玩笑的語氣來表達。

Stick a dagger in my heart!
在我心上用力地開一槍吧！

It's not rocket science
一點都不難

雖然不懂火箭科學是什麼，但一看就給人複雜又困難的感覺對吧？所以 It's not rocket science. 就是非常簡單，容易理解的意思。想要強調某件事「就跟 1+1 一樣簡單」的時候，就可以說這句話！但要注意的是，雖然這是一種幽默的表達方式，但有時也會帶給人負面感受。

Glenn	Yum! This is really delish. How did you make this?
Kayla	You just cook onions, carrots and celery in butter and add vegetable broth, chicken and noodles. Simmer it for about 20 min.
Glenn	This is so sweet of you.
Kayla	💬 **It's not rocket science.** It's super simple.
Glenn	Still it's too much of a hassle for you.
Kayla	No worries. Hope you get well soon!

葛倫	嗯！這好好吃！妳怎麼做的？
凱拉	只要用奶油煎一煎洋蔥、胡蘿蔔跟芹菜，再加入蔬菜湯、雞肉跟麵煨 20 分鐘就好。
葛倫	妳好用心。
凱拉	這一點都不難，非常簡單。
葛倫	但還是很麻煩妳。
凱拉	小事一樁，希望你早日康復！

SLANG **delish**

delish 是 delicious 的縮略語，雖然母語使用者也會說 delicious，不過也有更多其他常用的說法。

savory	awesome	amazing
可口的	很棒的	驚人的
great	**flavorful**	**tasty**
很棒的	美味的	好吃的
good	**mouthwatering**	**yummy**
好的	令人垂涎的	很好吃的

CULTURE **我們生病的時候會吃「粥」！美國人都吃什麼？**

美國人生病——尤其是感冒或是疲勞無力的時候，通常會吃「雞湯（chicken soup）」，就像我們生病時都會吃粥一樣。如果知道美國人有生病就喝雞湯的文化，那就不難懂多年來受到全球讀者喜愛的《心靈雞湯》（Chicken Soup for the Soul）取這個書名的用意了，看得出來這是一本意在療癒疲乏心靈的書。

EXPRESSION **「料理」的相關用語有哪些？**

simmer 意為「慢燉收乾水分」。也來認識一下其他料理基本用語吧！

grill	roast	chop	slice
火烤	烘烤	切段、切塊	切片
fry	**marinate**	**boil**	**steam**
炸、炒	用醬汁醃泡	煮沸	蒸
stir	**blend**	**grind**	**salt down**
攪拌、混合	混合	磨碎	用鹽醃

CULTURE **在美國探病時要帶什麼？**

在台灣探病時，大多會送水果籃，不過美國人通常會送寫有「Get well soon!」的卡片、氣球、熊娃娃或花束。在美國，只要去超市都能找到有這些商品的組合包。上網搜尋「Get well soon Teddy bear」、「Get well soon card」等關鍵字，看看它們長什麼樣子吧！「早日痊癒」也可以用 Hope you get well soon.。

I feel under the weather
我有點不舒服

可以用在身體狀況不適，或是有點不舒服的情形，有時也可表示做事提不起勁、心情不好的狀態。其他表達身體不適的症狀：<u>My body aches all over.</u>（我全身痠痛）；I have the chills.（我身體發冷）；I have a fever.（我發燒了）；I feel shaky.（我身體在打顫）等說法。

Anthony　You don't seem quite well. Are you feeling OK?

Lora　　💬 **I feel under the weather** a bit. I have a mild headache.

Anthony　You might have caught a cold.

Lora　　I shouldn't have swum last night, huh? It was really chilly.

安東尼　妳看起來不太舒服，妳還好嗎？

蘿拉　　我不太舒服，頭有點痛。

安東尼　妳可能感冒了。

蘿拉　　我昨晚不該游泳的，對吧？天氣太涼了。

「身體狀況不好」用英文怎麼說？

身體狀況不好這句話經常被直譯為 My body condition is not good.，其實這是非常不自然的表現。well 當作形容詞使用時代表「健康的」、「健康良好的」，正確的説法有 I don't feel well. 或 I'm unwell.。而 I feel good. 雖然也可以解釋為身體狀態好，不過大部分是用來表示「心情好」的意思。James Brown 不是有一首歌就叫〈I Feel Good〉嗎？

I'm feeling extremely unwell.
我身體很不舒服。

She is mentally unwell.
她心理狀態不太好。

GRAMMAR might have + p.p.

意指過去「可能（做過某事）」、「或許（做過某事）也不一定」，表示不確定但有可能的態度。近來 may have 及 might have 的用法幾乎相同，關於兩者差異，語言學家之間意見也有分歧。不過連接 if 子句表示與過去事實相反的假設，表達「原本可以（做某事），但最後沒有那麼做」的意思時要用 might have 才對。

I might have left my wallet at home.
我可能把錢包忘在家裡了。

If I could speak English, I might have tried going to school abroad.
要是我會講英文的話，應該會試著出國唸書。

GRAMMAR a cold?

在美式英文中，cold（感冒）、headache（頭痛）、stomachache（胃痛）、runny nose（流鼻水）、fever（發燒）、sore throat（喉嚨痛）等不嚴重的病症，因可能反覆發生，所以被分類為「可數名詞」，前面要加不定冠詞 a。

I have a runny nose and a slight fever.
我一直流鼻水，還有一點發燒。

不過被分類為 chronic disease（慢性病）的疾病或是例如「癌症」之類的重病，則被視為「不可數名詞」。

Steve Jobs suffered from pancreatic cancer.
賈伯斯受胰臟癌所苦。

EXPRESSION chilly

這裡的 chilly 可不是指辣醬 chilli sauce！跟形容詞 cold 一樣，有天氣或場所太涼或寒冷的意思，也用來指稱心理層面的感受，主詞為人的時候可以解釋為待人不親切或是冷漠。

His response was rather chilly.
他的反應很冷淡。

One for the road!

喝最後一杯再上路！

在上路（road）前，也就是離開前喝一杯（one），等同於「喝最後一杯再上路！」。雖然得回家，但是說服對方再喝最後一杯時，就可以說「Let's just have one more for the road.」。one 也可以換成 drink、bottle、can 或 shot，也可以用在非酒類的飲料或食物上。例如 I need some food for the road!（我需要帶點吃的上路！）、 I'm just gonna have one more can of beer for the road!（回家前我要再喝一杯啤酒！）。

Ken	Dang! I gotta go. Let's have  **one for the road**!
Jolie	What do you mean? The night is still young.
Ken	It's like walking on eggshells right now. My wife's gonna kill me.
Jolie	You suck!
Ken	I got so shit-faced last week, remember?
Jolie	Zip your lips! Bottoms up!

肯	啊！我該走了，讓我們喝最後一杯吧！
茱莉	你在說什麼啊？現在才傍晚而已。
肯	我現在如履薄冰，我老婆會殺了我的。
茱莉	你好差勁！
肯	我上禮拜喝個爛醉，妳忘了嗎？
茱莉	閉嘴！乾杯！

EXPRESSION **The night is young.**

直譯是「夜很年輕」，也就是夜還未深，「才傍晚」的意思。

The night is still young. Let's go for another bottle of wine!
現在才傍晚，我們再喝一瓶酒吧！

IDIOM **walking on eggshells**

eggshell 是「蛋殼」，walking on eggshells（走在蛋殼上）就是「如履薄冰」的意思，指為了不讓對方傷心或生氣，凡事小心謹慎、看對方的臉色。類似的用法還有 skating/walking on thin ice。

I've been walking on eggshells around Jenny since she recently got fired.
自從珍妮被解僱，在她身邊我都小心翼翼的。

SLANG **「喝醉、爛醉」用英文怎麼說？**

爛醉如泥只會用 very drunk 來形容嗎？

shit-face 是俚語，如果和對方不夠熟，建議還是不要使用，但是這個用法很常在電影或電視劇聽到，意為喝太多酒，醉得「像灘爛泥」一樣。

plastered
爛醉

trashed
爛醉（軟爛到可以丟到垃圾桶）

wasted
爛醉

black out
斷片，醉到昏過去

IDIOM **Zip your lips!**

zip 名詞是「拉鍊」，動詞是「拉起拉鍊」的意思。在這裡則是「閉嘴」、「不要再說了」等意思，可以簡單地說 Zip it! 或 Zip!。

I told John to zip it since he won't stop talking about nonsense.
我叫約翰閉嘴，因為他一直亂講話。

IDIOM **「乾杯」英文怎麼說？**

Bottoms up! 讓杯底朝上，也就是「一口氣喝乾」的意思。也可以用 Down the hatch!，hatch 是船進貨的「艙口」，比喻成嘴巴，一口氣灌入酒。另外，在喝酒前也可以說 Chin-chin!，當作祝福詞。

Don't bite off more than you can chew

別自不量力

「不要咬超過你能咀嚼的份量」也就是「不要太勉強或貪心」的意思。當對方設定的目標太高或承諾無法遵守的約定,又或者想做超出自己能力的事時,就可以對他說這句話。無論做什麼事,都要量力而為,持之以恆,才會成功。

Betty   I have made up my mind!

Dan   Elaborate.

Betty   I signed up for a gym and an English class. I'm also going to learn how to play the piano.

Dan   That sounds great but 💬 **don't bite off more than you can chew**. Take it slow, otherwise you fizzle out after a few days.

貝蒂   我下定決心了。

丹   説來聽聽。

貝蒂   我報名了健身房和英文課,而且我還要學鋼琴。

丹   很好啊,可是妳不要太勉強。慢慢來,不然沒多久就失敗了。

MOST CONFUSED · make up one's mind

make-up 是名詞，為「化妝」的意思，而 make up 是片語動詞，會根據上下文和情境有天差地遠的意思，最常看到的意思有「和好」、「捏造」、「決定」、「彌補」等，make up one's mind 則是「下定決心」的意思。

I made up with Anna.
我和安娜和好了。

I'll make it up to you. I'm sorry.
我會彌補你的，對不起。

She made that up!
那是她捏造的！

I need to take the make-up class.
我必須上重補修的課。

EXPRESSION · elaborate

當形容詞是「精緻」的意思；當動詞時，則如會話中的意思，主要當作「再說仔細點」的意思。

Could you elaborate on what you've just said?
你可以把剛剛說的內容再說仔細一點嗎？

EXPRESSION · Sounds great!

聽起來好聽？No! 這是「好點子！」、「好耶！」、「太好了！」、「不錯耶！」的意思。這樣的反應是會話的亮點，當對方告訴你好消息，或是問你他的意見如何，就可以這樣回應。sounds 後面可以試著接上各種形容詞哦！

A: I want hot pot for dinner. 晚餐我想吃火鍋。
B: Sounds fantastic! 好耶，超棒的！

IDIOM · fizzle out

意指原本滿懷希望和期待開始的事，漸漸不了了之。用來描述事情隨時間漸漸無力執行或以失敗收場，也可以用來形容碳酸飲料沒氣。

Our plans have fizzled out.
我們的計畫最後不了了之。

My feelings for Diana have fizzled out.
我對黛安娜的感情已冷。

Don't count your chickens before they hatch

別高興得太早

「別在小雞孵化前就數有幾隻」意為當還未有確切的結果出現時，不要預設一切都會很順利而小題大作。要注意，這個用法帶有負面的意味在哦。

Ethan	How was the job interview?
Elly	I think I got it. I should go shopping tomorrow for new clothes.
Ethan	Whoa whoa. Hold your horses. 💬 **Don't count your chickens before they hatch!**
Elly	I really think I made it!
Ethan	We'll see about that.

伊森	面試如何？
艾莉	我想我會上。明天我應該去添購新衣服。
伊森	哦！冷靜點，別高興得太早！
艾莉	我真的覺得我穩上！
伊森	到時候就知道了。

EXPRESSION **I got it.**

母語者經常把 I got it. 掛在嘴邊，根據上下文和情境會有各種不同的意思。got you 也可以說成 gotcha（我懂了／我明白了）。

I got it!
我懂了！／我買到了！／我接到了！／我知道了！／我來做！

I got this.
我行的！

EXCLAMATION **whoa whoa**

whoa 是感嘆或驚訝時使用的感嘆詞，同「哇！」但是會話中連續使用兩次，是為了讓某人冷靜下來的意思。這個用法原本用在讓馬停下來，也可以用在讓奔馳的馬冷靜下來。

IDIOM **Hold your horses.**

這是一句命令句，希望對方在做決定前，不要太興奮，暫時緩緩、慎重思考。有「你再等等」、「再多想想看」等意思。

Just hold your horses! This could be a life-changing decision.
不要太興奮，再想想看！這決定可能會改變你的人生。

EXPRESSION **I made it.**

該不會大家解釋成「我做的」吧？make 當動詞雖然是「製做」，但是也有「成功」、「實現」、「達成目標」等意思。因此 make it 可以解釋成「達成」、「做到」、「準時赴約」等。

Billie Eilish really made it as a singer.
「怪奇比莉」成功以歌手的身分走紅。

Do you think you can make it to my party?
你覺得你有辦法參加我的派對嗎？

EXPRESSION **We'll see.**

直譯為「我們將看到」，意思是「到時候就知道了」、「我們走著瞧」。

We'll see what happens.
我們就看會發生什麼事。

When it rains it pours

禍不單行

指壞事接連而來。通常我們會用「傾盆大雨」來形容雨下很大，英文則會說 It's pouring.，因此這個用法是「不雨則以，一雨傾盆」的意思，指當一件事情出錯，所有事情都會跟著出問題。人生在世，難免會遇到不幸接連來敲門，但是終究會雨過天晴的。This too shall pass!（一切都會過去的！）

Simon　It's been a long day today.

Alex　What happened? You look exhausted.

Simon　I got into a minor fender bender this morning. Obviously I was late for work. Last but not least, I tripped and sprained my ankle on my way home.

Alex　Holy moly Guacamole! 💬 **When it rains it really pours.**

賽門　今天真是漫長的一天。

艾莉克絲　怎麼了？你看起來很無力。

賽門　今天早上我發生了一點小擦撞，想當然上班就遲到了，而且最後精采的是我回家時還被絆倒，扭傷了我的腳踝。

艾莉克絲　我的老天鵝啊！你真是屋漏偏逢連夜雨耶！

EXPRESSION a long day

結束辛苦又疲憊的一天，我們常說真是「漫長的一天」。若是不好受，總覺得一天特別長。

It's been a long day without you, my friend.

沒有你的日子如此漫長，我的朋友。

摘自《玩命關頭》Charlie Puth 所演唱悼念 Paul Walker 保羅沃克的〈See You Again〉。

It's gonna be a long day tomorrow.

明天將會是漫長的一天。

IDIOM fender bender

意指「輕微的汽車擦撞」，也指因為不小心而經常引發小事故的駕駛。

Sarah is involved in a three-car fender bender. She said it's very minor though!

莎拉說他發生了三車擦撞的車禍，但是是很輕微的擦撞。

IDIOM last but not least

雖然是最後才提到，但是和前述提到的內容或人物同等重要，相當於「最後重要的是～」，這是頒獎典禮上必出現的用語。雖然會話中翻成「最後精彩的是」，但相當於「最後一擊」的意思。

Last but not least, I would like to thank my parents for their sacrifice and love.

最後也最重要的是，我要感謝我父母的犧牲和愛。

EXCLAMATION Holy moly Guacamole!

Holy moly! 和表達驚訝到難以置信的 Oh my God! 是一樣的感嘆詞。也可用 Holy cow、Holy shit、Holy crap 等用法，可解釋為「太酷了」、「天啊」、「太驚人了」等。Holy guacamole! 出自於電影《蝙蝠俠》，因為說法有趣而成為流行語，進一步還可以說 Holy moly Guacamole Ravioli!。Guacamole 是墨西哥酪梨醬、Ravioli 是義大利餃。

Holy moly! Are you serious?

什麼？！認真？

Holy cow! That's gigantic!

太驚人了！真的好大！

Holy moly Guacamole! Congrats!

天啊！恭喜你！

Holy shit! What the hell is that!?

哇！那到底是什麼啊？

Let's Practice!
DAY 21-30

請用題目中給的單字造句。

1. 他們好適合。（look）

2. 七轉八起。（stand up）

3. 他的反應很冷淡。（response）

4. 別自不量力。（bite off）

5. 一點也不難。（rocket）

6. 情人眼裡出西施。（in the eye of）

7. 別高興得太早。（before they hatch）

8. 你在説什麼屁話？（Where）

9. 喝最後一杯再上路！（road）

10. 把你的情緒發洩出來吧。（out of）

解答 1

1) They look good together. 2) Fall down seven times, stand up eight. 3) His response was chilly. 4) Don't bite off more than you can chew. 5) it's not rocket science. 6) Beauty lies in the eye of the beholder. 7) Don't count your chickens before they hatch. 8) Where is this coming from? 9) One for the road! 10) Get it out of your system.

Exercise 2　依照句意填入正確答案。

1. 希望你早日康復！

Get _____!

2. 我有點不舒服。

I feel _____ a bit.

3. 你想有所得，就勢必得有所犧牲。

You've got to _____.

4. 我下定決心了。

I made _____.

5. 禍不單行。

When it _____.

6. 今天是漫長的一天。

It's _____.

7. 我做到了。

I _____.

8. 乾杯！

_____ up!

9. 沒什麼損失。

It _____.

10. 你現在是小題大作。

You are blowing it _____.

解答 2

1) well soon　2) under the weather　3) crack a few eggs to make an omelet　4) up my mind
5) rains it pours　6) been a long day　7) made it　8) Bottoms　9) can't hurt　10) out of
proportion

In the wrong place at the wrong time

運氣不好

「在不對的時機,出現在不對的地方」,即「雖然並非刻意,但是卻偏偏在那個時候出現在有問題的地方」。

用在雖然沒做錯事,卻被捲入不好的事或發生意外的時候。相反地,In the right place at the right time. 則是「在對的時機,幸運地出現在對的地方」。

"The wrong guy, the wrong night, at the wrong time."
——拜登(Joe Biden)2020 大選辯論

Nancy I can't believe my phone got stolen! I hate it here now. I wanna go home!

Luis Take a chill pill. You were just  **in the wrong place at the wrong time**. Snap out of it. Come on! We are in Paris!

Nancy Sorry. I wasn't myself for a moment.

Luis It's OK. Let's keep your important belonging somewhere safe now.

南希 我不敢相信我的手機被偷了!我不想待在這裡,我要回家!

路易斯 冷靜。妳只是踩到狗屎,別想了。我們現在在巴黎耶!

南希 抱歉,我一時失去理智了。

路易斯 沒關係,之後把貴重物品放在安全的地方吧。

home vs. house

home 是「家」，指自己所屬，或感到安全、安心的場所。相反地，house 則是指「樓房」或「建築物」。因此「故鄉老友」叫做 homie；「鄉愁」叫做 homesick；「我美滿的家」叫做 sweet home；「故鄉」叫做 hometown。home 除了名詞，也可以當作副詞使用，意為「回家；到家」。當 home 作副詞使用時，不加上介系詞 to。

I'm at home. （名詞 home）
我在家。

I'm home! （副詞 home）
我到家了！

I bought a big house in Kinmen.
我在金門買了個大房子。

IDIOM Take a chill pill.

Take a chill pill.（吃點鎮定劑吧）和 Calm down. 是一樣的意思。chill 有「放輕鬆；游手好閒；玩樂；灑脫」等意思。類似表達還有 Chill out! 和 Just chill! 等。

Just chill out! Stop stressing over little things!
放輕鬆！不要糾結小事。

I'm just chilling at home.
我就只是在家休息。

IDIOM Snap out of it.

字面上的意思是「從那裡出來」，可以對陷入憂鬱、憤怒、負面情緒或煩惱的朋友，或是腦袋不清楚、做出無厘頭舉動的朋友說。有「加油」、「擺脫負面情緒吧」、「振作」等意思。

I couldn't snap out of depression.
我無法擺脫憂鬱情緒。

Please snap out of it! Stop thinking about it!
拜託別鑽牛角尖了！不要再想了！

Through thick and thin
同甘共苦

意為「無論在什麼情況下，我都會不吝支持和相伴」。結婚誓詞中有句「For better or worse」，意思就是無論是好是壞、順境或逆境（through good times and bad times），夫妻都要攜手共度，和 through thick and thin 的意思相近。

Siena	What happened to you and Morgan?
Kyle	I figured that he was a fair weather friend. I believe friends stick together 💬 **through thick and thin**.
Siena	Oh... sorry for bringing that up. I didn't know you guys are on bad terms.
Kyle	It's cool.

席安那	你和摩根發生什麼事啦？
凱爾	我覺得那傢伙只是個酒肉朋友，我認為朋友應該要能同甘共苦。
席安那	哦……抱歉，我不該提起的，我不知道你們關係不好。
凱爾	沒關係啦。

IDIOM **a fair weather friend**

只有天氣好的時候才是朋友,即「酒肉朋友」。指情況不錯的時候才能當朋友,但是當你落難或遇到困難的時候,卻無法支持你,是不值得信賴的人。

Don't waste your time on a fair weather friend.
不要把時間浪費在酒肉朋友身上。

EXPRESSION **bring (something/someone) up**

這個片語有「提起話題」、「撫養孩子」、「把什麼東西帶上來」等各種意思。在上述會話中,指很不識相提起不好的話題,而感到抱歉的意思。

Don't bring that up! I don't want to hear it.
不要提起那件事!我不想聽!

He was brought up by his grandparents.
他是爺爺奶奶帶大的。

Could you bring it up from the lobby?
你可以從大廳幫我把那個東西拿上來嗎?

IDIOM **on bad terms**

指和某人傷了和氣,或互有疙瘩、不再交談的狀態。相反地,關係很好就叫做 on good terms。

We ended on bad terms.
我們最後不歡而散。

I'm not really on good terms with him.
我和他的關係沒有很好。

SPOKEN ENGLISH **It's cool.**

如果要表達「沒關係」,大概 90% 的人都會想到 It's OK.。然而口語中,It's cool. 除了「很酷、很棒」之外的意思,也有會話中的用法,為「沒關係」、「好啊」的意思。We are cool. 除了「我們很棒」的意思之外,也可以解讀成「我們合好了」。

You accepted my apology, right? Are we cool now?
你會接受我的道歉對吧?現在我們之間沒事了吧?

Pizza? I'm cool with it.
披薩嗎?嗯,好啊。

It runs in the blood
與生俱來

也可以說 It runs in the family.，指一家人在個性、才能或外表等所有正面或負面特質上，皆有共通點的意思。因此可以解釋為「家族遺傳」、「有其父必有其子」。

Betty   John is a tall drink of water.

Leo   His sister is also really tall like a model. I guess  **it runs in the blood**.

Betty   Jenny is such a sweet girl. She is so down to earth.

Leo   I think kindness and sweetness also run in the family.

Betty   Not to mention their looks!

貝蒂   約翰又高又帥耶。

里奧   他妹妹也跟模特兒一樣修長，看來是基因加持吧。

貝蒂   珍妮真的很善良，而且平易近人。

里奧   親切和貼心應該也是家族遺傳吧。

貝蒂   更別說他們的外表了！

tall drink of water

意指「長得高，外表出眾，相當有魅力的人」。就像炎熱的日子裡，口渴地望著一杯清涼的水一樣，極具魅力。因此也可以說 cool drink of water。

Who is that tall drink of water?
那又高又帥的人是誰啊？

 sweet

你只知道 sweet 是「甜」的意思嗎？在口語中，sweet 可以用來表達很多不同的語意哦。

1 甜的

I'm craving something sweet.
我想吃點甜的。

2 貼心的

I always fall for sweet guys.
我每次都被貼心的男生吸引。

3 謝謝！（可用來取代 Thank you!）

Aww! How sweet!
哦！謝謝！

4 耶！太棒了！

A: We won the game! 我們贏了！
B: Sweet! 耶！太棒了！

 down to earth

指「務實、樸素，不擺架子的人」，用來稱讚即使擁有得很多、很成功，仍懂得謙虛的人。

Warren Buffett is so down to earth compare to what he has.
華倫巴菲特過得比他所擁有的還樸素。

EXPRESSION not to mention

「更別說～，當然」的意思。後面可以和名詞、形容詞、動名詞連用。

Not to mention her beauty!
更別說她有多美！

Not to mention expensive!
貴是當然的！

He is a bad apple!

他是顆老鼠屎！

「不正直又帶來負面影響的人」被稱作 a bad apple（壞蘋果）或 rotten apple（爛蘋果），源自於美國的諺語「A bad apple spoils the bunch.」（一顆老鼠屎壞了一鍋粥），意為因為一個人不好的行為，連帶讓其身邊的人都受到一樣的誤解或被帶壞。

Megan	Andrew is a total rat. I freaking hate him.
Lewis	There is no doubt that 💬 **he is a bad apple.**
Megan	Kyle used to be the sweetest guy but not anymore after hanging out with Andrew.
Lewis	Duh! A bad apple spoils the bunch.
Megan	So, you always have to surround yourself with good people.

梅根	安德魯根本是騙子，討厭死了。
路易斯	無須懷疑，他就是個壞人。
梅根	凱爾是我見過最善良的人，但自從他和安德魯來往後，就不再是了。
路易斯	妳現在才知道嗎？近朱者赤，近墨者黑。
梅根	所以我們都要和好人來往。

SLANG rat

「愛告密、打小報告，不值得信任的人」稱為 rat（老鼠），指騙子或叛徒。而 smell a rat 則有「感覺可疑」、「察覺事有蹊蹺」等意思。

I smell a rat. John wouldn't ask me for money.
感覺有點可疑，約翰不會向我要錢的。

SLANG freaking

freaking 在此為副詞，是「非常、很、極為」的意思，屬於非正式用語。freaking 是 fucking 的委婉表現，無論男女老少皆可使用。

It's freaking cold! 超冷的！
I'm freaking busy these days. 我最近很忙。
Freaking be quiet! 拜託安靜！

MOST MISTAKEN hang out

台灣人最常犯的英文錯誤之一就是「和朋友玩」，通常會說成 I played with my friend.，此為錯誤說法。play 指小孩子玩扮家家酒，用在成人是 18 禁色色的「玩」！「和朋友玩」的正確說法是 hang out，可別忘囉！

I hung out with my friend in Hollywood last night.
我昨天晚上和朋友在好萊塢玩。

Where do you usually hang out?
你通常都在哪裡活動啊？

EXCLAMATION Duh!

當對方不知道一件非常理所當然的事時，可以用這個感嘆詞來表達「這還用說嗎？」、「你連這都不知？」，有時帶有「你是笨蛋嗎？」輕蔑的意思。

Duh! You didn't know that?
那不是理所當然的嗎？你不知道嗎？

Duh! I'm not stupid!
這還用說嗎？我又不是笨蛋！

Don't beat yourself up
別自責

---

beat up 「毆打、毒打」，不要毒打你自己，即「別自責」的意思。也就是說對於失敗或犯錯，不要過度責怪或歸咎於自己。類似的用法還有 self-bullying、self-criticizing，或 Don't be so hard on yourself.。

Son　Mom, I'm sorry for breaking the promise.

Mom　Apology accepted, but you really need to live up to your words.

Son　You have my word this time. I had nightmares after the fight we had.

Mom　💬 **Don't beat yourself up.** I'm not gonna lay a guilt trip on you.

兒子　媽，抱歉，我沒遵守約定。

媽媽　我接受你的道歉，但是你必須說話算話。

兒子　這次妳可以相信我。和妳吵架之後，我做了惡夢。

媽媽　別自責。我不會讓你有罪惡感的。

MOST MISTAKEN **promise**

promise 當動詞為「保證、承諾」之意，名詞則為「誓言」。當形容詞 promising 為保證成功的可能性，延伸為「有希望的、有前途的」。

Sorry. I can't promise you.
抱歉，我不敢保證。

She is a very smart girl with a promising future.
她是個聰明的女生，一定會有大好前途。

EXPRESSION **live up to your words**

live up to (something) 是「達到、符合（某事）」，通常有「不負寄望」的意思。因此 live up to your words. 就是「你要說話算話」，即「遵守自己說過的話」。

The movie lived up to everyone's expectation.
那部電影符合所有人的期待。

The president lived up to his promise.
總統遵守了他的承諾。

He surely lives up to his reputation.
他為人處世不愧對自己的名聲。

EXPRESSION **You have my word.**

給對方自己的話，就是「我向你承諾」，同 I promise you.，兩者語氣對母語人士來說，承諾的強度差不多。

Do you give your word on it?
你可以保證嗎？

I'll give you my word.
我答應你。

IDIOM **guilt trip**

guilt 是「罪惡感」，trip 則為「旅行」的意思，但跟旅行無關，而是「強烈愧疚」的意思。也可以當作動詞使用，意為平白無故讓對方覺得愧疚、有罪惡感。

名詞

He lays a guilt trip on me about everything.
他讓我對一切感到非常愧疚。

動詞

Stop guilt tripping me!
不要再讓我有罪惡感了！

A picture is worth a thousand words
百聞不如一見

這個用法和我們的諺語「百聞不如一見」意思類似。最近常能在香菸包裝上看到警告吸菸的圖，根據報告顯示，這種讓人感到不舒服的圖片比調漲香菸價格、用標語傳遞資訊來的更有效。像這樣將訊息視覺化使人親眼看到，讓人更能直覺地接收訊息，容易理解和加深記憶。用英語來表達就可以說 A picture is worth a thousand words. 或 A picture paints a thousand words.。

Hector　Where do you recommend traveling in Korea?

Lora　If you are looking for a historical place, I recommend Gyeongju. It is just beyond words.

Hector　I heard it's like an open air museum.

Lora　💬 **A picture paints a thousand words.**
Just go! You won't regret it.

Hector　Thanks, Lora.

Lora　No biggie!

海特　去韓國旅行，妳會推薦我去哪裡？

蘿拉　如果你想找有歷史情懷的地方，我會推薦慶州，我很難用言語向你形容。

海特　我聽說那裡就像露天博物館。

蘿拉　百聞不如一見。去就對了！你絕不會後悔。

海特　謝啦，蘿拉。

蘿拉　不會！

MOST CONFUSED **historical vs. historic**

像上述會話中，能呈現過去歷史的場所或遺跡，就用 historical 來形容；而具有歷史意義，象徵歷史性的一刻、難忘的紀錄、歷史事件等，就會使用 historic。

Rome has many historical sites like Tainan.
羅馬像台南一樣，有很多歷史遺跡。

It was a historic moment when Obama became the first African-American president of the United States of America.
歐巴馬成為美國第一位黑人總統，是歷史性的一刻。

IDIOM **beyond words**

超乎言語，即「無法言喻的美好」。類似說法還有 beyond description，意為「不可勝言」、「難以形容的美好」。

Your beauty is beyond words.
你的美難以言喻。

EXPRESSION **open air museum**

本來是指露天博物館，後指到處都看得到遺址的「古蹟城市」，如羅馬整座城市就像露天博物館，一切都是藝術品。

SLANG **No biggie!**

No big deal. 的口語說法，是「沒什麼」的意思，可以用來取代我們都很熟悉的 You're welcome.（不客氣）。此外，還有 Don't mention it. / Don't worry about it. / No worries. / It's all good. / No problem. / It's nothing. 等說法。

A: Thanks for letting me borrow 20 bucks.
謝謝你借我 20 元美金。

B: No biggie. Anytime!
沒什麼，有需要隨時跟我說！

Ignorance is bliss
無知即是福

「無知即是幸福」，即「有些東西不必知道，這樣反而對精神健康比較好」的意思。因為如果知道了反而會擔心或影響心情，一點好處也沒有。

Jess Why don't we have Mickey D's for dinner?

Lora Have you seen the documentary about McDonald's?

Jess Jesus Christ! Do you hear yourself? I'm just trying to have a quick peaceful dinner.

Lora You may say 💬 **ignorance is bliss**, but actually knowledge is power.

Jess Knock it off! I'm having combo number 2!

傑思 我們晚餐吃麥當當如何？

蘿拉 你有看過關於麥當勞的紀錄片嗎？

傑思 天啊！妳在說什麼啊？我只是想要快點吃頓方便的晚餐而已。

蘿拉 雖然你一定覺得無知即是福，但實際上知識就是力量。

傑思 夠了，我要吃二號餐！

SLANG **Mickey D's**

就像台灣人會叫 McDonald's「麥當當」，美國人也會暱稱 Mickey D's。英國稱為 Maccy D's；澳洲的麥當勞招牌甚至寫成 Macca's。

EXCLAMATION **Jesus Christ!**

Jesus Christ 雖然是「耶穌」的意思，但是口語上作為感嘆詞，用在受到驚嚇、生氣、無奈、煩躁、無言的時候，和 Oh my God! 是一樣的意思。雖然這個用法無關宗教，任何人都可以用，但有時還是會有虔誠基督徒感到過敏哦！

Jesus Chris! You scared the heck out of me!
天啊！要被你嚇死了啦！

EXPRESSION **Do you hear yourself?**

直譯為「你有聽到你自己說的話嗎？」，實際是「你到底在說什麼啊？」的意思。也就是反問對方，有發現自己說的很牽強、不合理嗎？也可以說 Are you listening to yourself?。

Trump: Hilary and Obama created ISIS!
川普：希拉蕊和歐巴馬創造了 ISIS！

People: Do you even hear yourself...?
人民：你要不要聽聽自己說了什麼……？

PROVERB **Knowledge is power.**

正如字面上的意思，即「知識就是力量」。

Knowledge is power. But you must convert knowledge into action!
知識就是力量，但是一定要將知識身體力行！

IDIOM **knock it off!**

當你覺得對方很煩、想叫他閉嘴的時候，就可以說這句話。又或者某個人在胡說八道或說謊時，這句話也可以當成「屁啦」、「不要說那種話」的意思。

Knock it off! I don't want to hear your excuses!
閉嘴！我不想聽你狡辯！

Knock it off, kids! Stop running around!
孩子們，夠了哦！不要再跑來跑去了！

You can't have your cake and eat it too

魚與熊掌不可兼得

字面上是「你想吃蛋糕就無法擁有它，妳想擁有它就無法吃掉它。」即「你不可能擁有一切，也不可能同時喜歡兩邊的東西。」如同明星想獲得人氣，就得放棄自由；為了獲得財富，人們也會放棄人際關係。有得必有失，這是永恆的真理。

Sarah I'm so jealous of you. I wish I could work for myself too.

Leon You have a stable job. Stable income which I don't have!

Sarah I guess it's like comparing apples to oranges.

Leon Everything has its pros and cons. Nothing is perfect in this world.

Sarah Yeah, 💬 **you can't have your cake and eat it too.**

莎拉　　我真羨慕你。我也希望我是老闆。

里昂　　妳有穩定的工作啊，我就沒有穩定的薪水！

莎拉　　我想這種比較太沒意義了。

里昂　　任何事情有優點也有缺點，世界上沒有任何一件事是完美的。

莎拉　　沒錯，魚與熊掌不可兼得。

MOST ASKED jealous

「我好羨慕你」英文雖然可以說 I envy you.，但 envy 比 jealous 語氣更強烈，80% 以上的美國人會說 I'm jealous.，或俚語 I'm so jelly.。不過要注意 jealous 是形容詞，後面必須加介系詞 of。

I'm so jealous of his humility.
我好羨慕他的謙卑。

Wow! You got into Harvard? I'm so jelly!
哇！你上哈佛了？好羨慕哦！

EXPRESSION work for myself

「為了自己工作」就是「自由工作者」的意思。這是母語人士自我介紹時，經常派上用場的句子。類似的說法還有 self-employed。

Billy works for himself. He is a YouTuber.
比利是自由工作者，他是 YouTuber。

IDIOM compare apples to oranges

把蘋果跟橘子拿來比，是在比較種類、味道、口感截然不同的水果，即「風馬牛不相及」、「不能相提並論」。另外，形容天差地遠、截然不同的兩者，英文也會比喻成 apples and oranges。

Comparing Jazz and classical music is comparing apples to oranges.
爵士樂和古典樂完全不一樣，無法比較。

They are twins but apples and oranges.
他們雖然是雙胞胎，但是太不一樣了。

EXPRESSION Everything has its pros and cons.

「所有事物皆有優缺點」的意思。源自於拉丁語的 pro et contra，相當於 for and against（支持與反對）。注意 pros and cons 並不能拆開。單獨說法有：優點 advantage、strength；缺點 disadvantage、flaw 等。

You need to weigh the pros and cons before making the decision.
下決定前，你必須先衡量優缺點。

The pros outweigh the cons.
優點大於缺點。

There are plenty of fish in the sea

天涯何處無芳草

海裡有很多魚！即「這世界有很多機會和各種選擇權」的意思。通常這句話是對在愛情上遇到一些挫折，或因為分手而心痛的朋友說，意思是這世界上男人或女人這麼多，不要再難過了。

Gabriel   Emily friend zoned me again.

Lora   You still have a crush on her?

Gabriel   It's her third time turning me down.

Lora   It's really time to move on, Gabriel.
        💬 **There are plenty of fish in the sea!**

加百列   艾蜜莉又發給我好人卡了。

蘿拉   你還在暗戀她？

加百列   這是她第三次拒絕我了。

蘿拉   加百列，你真的該放手了。天涯何處無芳草啊！

EXPRESSION **friend zone**

zone 當作名詞是「區域」的意思，當作動詞則是「指定某個區域做特定的事」。因此 friend zone 一般都當作動詞使用，指和無法發展成戀人的劃清界線，當朋友就好。

I get friend zoned by every crush.
我一直被我喜歡的人發好人卡。

 IDIOM **have a crush on somebody**

指暗戀某個人，即「單戀」。crush 當作名詞時，也有「暗戀對象」的意思。

I've had a crush on Jenny for 3 years.
三年來我一直暗戀珍妮。

He is my crush from high school.
他是我高中時期的暗戀對象。

 EXPRESSION **turn down (someone/something)**

turn down 有「拒絕；摺（被子等）；降低音量」等意思。

I got turned down for a job.
我面試工作被刷掉了。

Can I get a turn-down service?
可以幫我整理（飯店）房間和床嗎？

Could you please turn down the volume?
你可以把聲音調低嗎？

 EXPRESSION **move on**

move on 雖然是「跳到下個階段」的意思，但是在上述會話中 move on 是「忘記過去，重新出發」的意思。如果你的朋友忘不了舊情人而痛苦，或是被困在過去、裹足不前，就可以使用這個用法。

I'm going to move on. I'm going to meet someone now.
我決定忘掉他了，我現在要去見新對象。

Let's move on to the next topic.
讓我們進到下個主題吧。

Day 39

There is no such thing as a free lunch

天下沒有白吃的午餐

「天下沒有白吃的午餐」就是「任何事都不是免費的」。當你想強調,如果想得到某個東西,就要付出等值的努力,就可以使用這句話。這世界上哪有能免費獲得的東西啊?如果你知道這項真理,就會更努力生活,不依賴僥倖。

Matt   I'm thinking of getting a loan to buy a new car.

Lora   Shut up! I thought your credit score was too low to get an auto loan.

Matt   I found this financial service for bad credit.

Lora   💬 **There is no such thing as a free lunch!**

Matt   Right. I got swayed by fake ads.

Lora   Get your act together! It doesn't matter what car you drive but who you are inside that matters.

麥特   我在想是不是要貸款買新車。

蘿拉   別說不切實際的話了!我想你的信用評分已經低到無法貸款了。

麥特   我已經找到為了信用不良者設計的金融產品了。

蘿拉   天下沒有白吃的午餐!

麥特   也是,我被不實廣告給迷惑了。

蘿拉   振作點!開什麼車不重要,重要的是你的本質!

PATTERN I'm thinking of + 動名詞／名詞

這是「我在想……」的句型，後面可以接動名詞或名詞。

I'm thinking of having pasta for dinner.
我在想晚餐要不要吃義大利麵。

I'm always thinking of you.
我一直在想你。

SPOKEN ENGLISH Shut up!

你以為 Shut up! 只有「閉嘴！」的意思嗎？其實 Shut up! 也有「別搞笑了」、「別説不切實際的話」的意思，也可以當作「不可置信」的感嘆詞使用。

What? Shut up! Oh my God. I can't believe this.
什麼？不可能！天啊，我不敢相信。

EXPRESSION get swayed by

受人、情緒等「控制；影響擺布」。

Don't get swayed by your emotions but learn to discipline and contain them.
不要被你的情緒影響，你得學會克制和管理的方法。

Jenny got swayed by his sweet talks.
珍妮被他的甜言蜜語擺布。

IDIOM Get your act together!

「振作起來！」好好工作、好好生活的意思。也有整理好身邊的事，調整好自己的精神的意思。

He got his act together and got a job.
他振作起來，找到了一份工作。

You will have to get your act together if you want to meet the deadline.
如果你想在截止日前完成，就振作起來好好做。

Let's Practice!
DAY 31-40

Exercise 1 請用題目中給的單字造句。

1. 他是顆老鼠屎。（bad）

2. 你得説話算話。（live）

3. 夠了。（knock）

4. 天下沒有白吃的午餐。（There is no such thing）

5. 別説不切實際的話了！（up）

6. 把一切都忘了重新開始吧！（on）

7. 魚與熊掌不可兼得。（your cake）

8. 百聞不如一見。（A picture is worth）

9. 運氣不好。（In the wrong place）

10. 與生俱來。（It runs）

解答 1

1) He is a bad apple.　2) Live up to your words.　3) knock it off.　4) There is no such thing as free lunch.　5) Shut up! 6) Move on!　7) You can't have your cake and eat it too.　8) A picture is worth a thousand words.　9) In the wrong place at the wrong time.　10) It runs in the blood.

1. 我們總是同甘共苦。

We've been through _____.

2. 冷靜點。

Take _____.

3. 她真的很謙遜。

She is _____.

4. 物以類聚。

Birds _____.

5. 天涯何處無芳草。

There are _____.

6. 我好羨慕你。

I'm _____.

7. 無知便是福。

_____ bliss.

8. 這無法言喻。

It is _____.

9. 別自責。

Don't _____.

10. 他只是個酒肉朋友。

He was a _____.

解答 2

1) thick and thin   2) a chill pill   3) down to earth   4) of a feather flock together   5) plenty of fish in the sea   6) jealous of you   7) Ignorance is   8) beyond words   9) beat yourself up
10) fair weather friend

It is music to my ears!

真是個好消息！

當聽到如音樂般美好的消息時可以使用的句子，相當於「眾多消息中的好消息」、「太好了」、「期待已久、太想聽到的話」。類似的用法還有 I'm happy to hear that. 和 Good to hear that. 等。如果讀者覺得這本書有趣又有幫助，我一定會大聲呼喊：「Thank you! That is music to my ears!」。

Sally	I'm leaving Ken. I'm dead serious this time.
Peter	💬 **That is music to my ears!** Thank God! Are you sure this time though?
Sally	Yes, I'm 100% positive.
Peter	Good! Once a cheater always a cheater.
Sally	I shouldn't have given him a second chance.
Peter	You deserve so much better.

莎莉	我要離開肯，我這次是說真的。
彼得	真是好消息！謝天謝地！妳這次真的確定了嗎？
莎莉	對，我百分之百確定。
彼得	很好！一日渣男，終身渣男。
莎莉	我不該給他機會的。
彼得	妳值得更好的。

EXPRESSION dead serious

serious 是「認真、嚴肅」的意思。雖然要強調「非常」的時候，可以用 very、extremely 等副詞，但是母語者會習慣加上 dead（死的），經常以此表達「跟死一樣認真」。

He is dead serious about working in New York.
他是真的很認真看待在紐約工作這件事。

EXCLAMATION Thank God!

「感謝上帝！」為非常開心、感激時的感嘆詞。有「幸好」、「太好了」、「真的太感謝」等意思。

Thank God it's Friday! (TGIF)
感謝上帝，終於星期五了！

EXPRESSION I'm positive.

這裡的 positive 不是「正面」的意思！I'm positive. 等於 I'm sure. 和 I'm certain. 的意思，表達「我確定、我確信」之意。加上 100% 有更強調的意思。

I'm positive! I saw it with my own eyes.
我確定！我親眼看到的。

IDIOM Once a cheater always a cheater.

cheater 雖然是「騙子」的意思，但是大部分用來指「劈腿的人」。意為只要劈腿一次，就會有下次。可以使用「Once a ～ always a ～」這個句型，表示人不會改變的意思。

Once a Marine always a Marine!
一日海軍陸戰隊，終身海軍陸戰隊！

EXPRESSION give (someone) a second chance

「給某人二次機會」就等於即使對方犯錯，也會原諒的意思。又或是如字面上，因為相信對方的能力，所以再給予二次機會的意思。

Everyone deserves a second chance.
所有人都擁有獲得二次機會的資格。

Can we take a rain check?

可以延到下次嗎？

這句話是源自於棒球比賽遇到下雨天而延賽的情形，因此這句話主要作為「下次吧」、「下次再約吧」的意思，用於遇到無法馬上答應對方的邀請或提議。也可以省略成問句 Rain check?。

Husband	Honey! Let's fly to Miami this weekend.
Wife	Sounds like a plan but  **can we take a rain check?**
Husband	Why? We have a 3-day weekend!
Wife	I hate to break it to you but we are short on cash this month.
Husband	Oh, I didn't know that.
Wife	Yeah, we have to tighten our belts.

老公	親愛的！我們這個週末飛邁阿密吧。
老婆	是不錯啦，但是我們可以下次再去嗎？
老公	為什麼？我們有三天的週末假期耶！
老婆	雖然我不想潑你冷水，但是這個月我們的錢不太夠。
老公	哦，我不知道。
老婆	嗯，我們得勒緊褲帶了。

PATTERN **fly to ＋（目的地）**

fly 意為「飛」，指搭飛機前往某處。這個用法可在機場 check in 的時候使用。另外，That's fly. 等同於 That's cool. 或 That's awesome.（超酷），但現在已經不常用了。

A: **Where are you flying to?** 您要飛往哪裡呢？
B: **I'm flying to Los Angeles.** 我要去洛杉磯。

EXPRESSION **Sounds like a plan.**

字面上是「聽起來像個計畫」，回應對方提議不錯、表示同意，即「這點子不錯耶」、「好啊，就這麼辦」。

A: **Do you want pizza for dinner? What do you say?** 晚上要不要吃披薩？如何？
B: **Sounds like a plan!** 好啊！

EXPRESSION **I hate to break it to you**

當要告訴對方不好的消息，或是要說的話難以啟齒時，就可以說這句，意為「雖然我也不想這麼說」、「雖然這麼說很抱歉」，後面則接想說的話。

I hate to break it to you but I'm not in love with you anymore.
雖然我不想說這種話，但是我不愛你了。

EXPRESSION **short on cash**

這個表達不是「錢很短」的意思，而是「錢不夠」，也可以換句話說 short on budget（預算不足）、short of money（錢不夠）等。

IDIOM **tighten our belts**

相當於中文的「勒緊褲頭」，意為「錢要省著點花」。

We have no choice but to tighten our belts a little more.
我們除了勒緊褲頭，省著花錢之外，別無選擇。

Save for a rainy day
未雨綢繆

「為了下雨天存錢」就是人生在世，難免會有始料未及的困難找上門，為了防範未然，平時就要省點錢儲蓄才行。Keep for a rainy day. 也是「存錢以備不時之需」的意思。

Peter	Hey, can I borrow 200 bucks?
Joe	Again? Are you saving at all?
Peter	Save? YOLO, man! Look at my new Rollie. FLEX!
Joe	You really need to start 💬 **saving for a rainy day**.
Peter	You know how much I make.
Joe	I know you make a lot of dough but life sometimes throws you a curveball.

彼得	喂，我可以跟妳借 200 美金嗎？
喬	又要借？你有在儲蓄嗎？
彼得	儲蓄？老兄，請活在當下！妳看我的新勞力士，炫耀一下！
喬	你應該存點錢以備不時之需。
彼得	妳知道我賺多少吧。
喬	我知道你賺很多，但是人生偶爾會出現你意想不到的事。

MOST CONFUSED · borrow vs. lend

一般人最常搞混的單字之一就是 borrow 和 lend 的差異。borrow 是「借入」，lend 是「借出」。因此，borrow 會和介系詞 from 連用（從誰那裡借入），lend 會和介系詞 to 連用（借給誰）。

Can I borrow a pen (from you)?
你可以借我一枝筆嗎？

Kevin borrowed my laptop (from me).
凱文把我的筆電借走了。

I lent 100 dollars to him.
我借他 100 元美金。

I never lend money to anyone.
我不會借錢給任何人。

SLANG · bucks

dollar（美元）的俚語，其他口語說法還有 dough，雖然是「麵粉」的意思，但因為麵包是主食，而麵包又是麵粉做的，所以引申為「錢」的意思。bread 也有「生計」的意思。

This is my bread and butter.
這是我謀生的飯碗。

SLANG · YOLO

You Only Live Once（你一生只活一次）的首字母縮寫。如同拉丁文 Carpe diem（活在今朝），即把握當下，及時享樂。

SLANG · Rollie

Rollie 是名牌勞力士（Rolex）手錶的簡稱。

SLANG · flex

flex 的原意是「使肌肉緊繃，展現肌肉」，最近常被當作「炫耀」、「展現」的意思。類似的說法還有 show off 和 boast。

A lot of guys flex their muscles in front of the mirror.
很多男生喜歡在鏡子前面大秀自己的肌肉。

IDIOM · life throws a curveball

curveball 是曲球，棒球的非直球難以擊中，引申為「意想不到的事或騙局」。因此，可以表達「人生中發生的意外、難關」。

When life throws a curveball, focus on what you can control.
當人生發生意想不到的難關時，那就專注在你能控制的事情上。

Burn bridges
自斷後路

這個表達源自於戰爭中將橋炸毀，因為這麼做通常是因為害怕而想逃亡，以及阻絕敵人，現今多用來形容說出或做出無法挽回的話或行動。Don't burn bridges. 即「別自斷後路」的意思。

Jason　I'm so quitting my job.

Lora　What? You were on fire!

Jason　My boss is a real jerk. He humiliated me in front of everyone.

Lora　That's a low blow.

Jason　I just wanted to flip him off and leave right there.

Lora　Still don't 💬 **burn bridges** like that. Let's cool off your anger first.

傑森　我要離職。

蘿拉　什麼？你不是很喜歡那份工作嗎？

傑森　我老闆真的很機車。他居然當眾羞辱我。

蘿拉　那真的很糟糕。

傑森　我當下真想給他一根中指轉頭就走。

蘿拉　但你別自斷後路，先冷靜平息怒火。

IDIOM **on fire**

如字面上，有「著火」的意思，但是也可以當作「熱情燃燒」，也就是「非常認真」的意思。on fire 也跟 hot 一樣，可以當作「性感」的意思使用。

She is on fire. She never sleeps.
她真的很拚，都不睡覺的。

You are looking on fire!
你好辣！

SLANG **jerk**

jerk 是指卑鄙自私，無禮又惹人厭的人，通常用在男人身上。

Dan is the biggest jerk I know. He is super narrow-minded and rude.
丹是我認識最爛的人了，他心胸超狹窄又沒禮貌。

IDIOM **low blow**

運動術語，指攻擊腰部以下的犯規，在一般日常用語指「卑鄙、小心眼的手段」，如羞辱對方、攻擊對方弱點、揭人瘡疤等。

Leaving vicious comments out of jealousy is a real low blow.
因為嫉妒就留惡評是相當卑鄙的行為。

IDIOM **flip (someone) off**

比中指，用手勢罵人的意思。和 fuck you 的意思相同。

The driver honked crazy and flipped me off.
那個駕駛瘋狂對我按喇叭，還比我中指。

EXPRESSION **cool off**

「使變冷」、「冷卻」的意思。除了字面上降溫的意思，也可用在情侶吵架，讓雙方靜一靜，平息怒火。

I'm gonna shower to cool off.
我要去沖澡降溫。

We are in a cool-off period.
我們現在正在讓彼此冷靜一段期間。

Don't judge a book by its cover
不要以貌取人

不要以一本書的封面來判斷內容好不好，也就是說「不要光憑眼前所見，就恣意下評斷」的意思。希望大家都不要以外表、擁有的東西和膚色來輕易評斷一個人，畢竟眼前所見，僅是冰山一角。

Mat　Did you know Kim's parents own The Palms hotel in Las Vegas?

Lora　Never in a million years since she pinches pennies all the time.

Mat　Tell me about it! It's really 💬 **don't judge a book by its cover**, huh?

Lora　Speaking of which, do you remember Alex?

Mat　All tattooed and scary looking guy?

Lora　Yeah, he turned out to be the most tender person.

麥特　妳知道金的爸媽在拉斯維加斯有一間棕櫚飯店嗎？

蘿拉　根本想不到，因為她是如此一毛不拔。

麥特　就是啊！真的是人不可貌相，對吧？

蘿拉　講到這裡，你記得艾力克斯嗎？

麥特　妳說全身刺青、看起來很兇的那個人嗎？

蘿拉　對！結果他是我見過心最軟的人了。

IDIOM **never in a million years**

過了一百萬年也絕對不，就是「門兒都沒有」、「絕不可能」、「無論如何都不會發生」。本來的用法是 not in a million years，但是改成 never 有強調的意思。

I never in a million years expected this to happen.
我從未想到會發生這種事。

IDIOM **pinch pennies**

penny（便士）就是 1 cent（1 分錢）。pinch 為「捏」的意思，也就是把 1 分錢緊握手裡，捨不得花。因此「小氣鬼」被稱作 penny pincher。

The couple had to pinch pennies after getting married.
那對夫妻結婚後就過得很省。

EXPRESSION **Tell me about it!**

字面上是「告訴我那件事」，也有「就是說啊」、「是不是」，表達「我也有同感」。

A: I can't wait for Christmas. 好希望聖誕節快來。
B: Tell me about it! I'm so excited! 就是啊！我好興奮！

EXPRESSION **speaking of somebody/something**

「既然講到這個」的意思，當聊到某人／事物，要順帶一提相關訊息，就可以使用這個表達。對話中的 which 代表前面說的「別以貌取人」這件事。

Speaking of Lora, she is a great teacher.
講到蘿拉，她真的是位好老師。

Speaking of summer, we should plan our vacation now.
講到夏天，我們該計劃度假的事了。

EXPRESSION **tender**

這個字可形容肉質「柔嫩」，但是也可以用來指一個人「心軟、敏感易受傷」。

This steak is so tender.
這牛排好嫩。

I'm sick of it!
我受夠了！

已經討厭到有壓力且覺得痛苦的「受不了」。比較單純的説法是 I'm tired of it.，可以解釋為「厭倦」的意思。sick of 後面可以使用各種名詞和動名詞，當有什麼事情讓你感到厭煩且疲倦的時候，可以活用看看這個用法。

Boyfriend Are you texting a guy?

Girlfriend Oh, please! Cut it out! That's it. Let's break up.

Boyfriend What do you mean?

Girlfriend 💬 **I'm sick of it!** I'm sick of fighting! I can't take this anymore.

Boyfriend I thought we put everything behind us.

Girlfriend Exactly. But obviously you still don't trust me.

男友　妳在傳簡訊給男人嗎？

女友　拜託！夠了哦！算了，我們分手吧。

男友　妳是什麼意思？

女友　我受夠了！我受夠了吵架，我無法再繼續了。

男友　我以為過去的事都過去了。

女友　沒錯！但是顯然你還是不信任我。

IDIOM **Cut it out!**

「夠了！」的意思，對方的行為讓你感到不悅，或你不想聽他說話時使用。「不要再說鬼話」可以說 Cut the crap.，crap 是「大便」，注意這個字不是正式用語喔。

Stop making stupid dad jokes! Cut it out!
停止那愚蠢的冷笑話！夠了！

Cut the crap! I don't believe anything you say.
不要再說謊了！我根本不相信你說的話。

EXPRESSION **I can't take this anymore.**

「我無法再忍耐了」。請記住，take 也有「忍耐、忍受」的意思喔！類似的用法還有 I can't stand something / someone.。

I can't take him anymore. He yaps nonstop.
我再也受不了那個人了，他一直講不停。

I can't stand this weather! It's way too cold!
我受不了這天氣了！冷死了！

IDIOM **put (something) behind**

「把一切拋諸腦後」，即「忘掉不好的回憶、爭執等事，當作事情沒發生過」的意思。

I'm just going to put all this behind me and just focus on the future.
我打算把這一切都忘掉，專注在未來上。

EXPRESSION **exactly**

「沒錯」、「一定」、「毫無疑問」的意思。當你完全認同對方說的話時，就可以用這個字來回應。

I know exactly how you feel.
我完完全全懂你的感受。

What exactly do I need to do?
確切來說我應該要做什麼？

A: Are you going out with Kyle? 你和凱爾在交往嗎？

B: Um, not exactly. It's actually just a fling. 嗯……不算。其實只是玩玩。

Haste makes waste

欲速則不達

如果急著做什麼事，最後就會導致一連串的失誤，而浪費了時間、努力、物質等。冰島俗語中有一句「神創造了時間，人類創造了焦急」，無論處在什麼情況中，還是要保持平常心，每件事都慎重決定後再行動吧。

Hailey	Guess what! I'm getting married in 2 weeks!
Ben	What? You just met John. What's the rush?
Hailey	Well, I'm in my middle 30s and I think he's my Mr. Right.
Ben	Age doesn't matter! And 💬 **haste makes waste**.
Hailey	I'm serious! He is the one.
Ben	Oh my God. You are so blinded by love!

海莉	我跟你說！我兩週後要結婚了！
班	什麼？妳跟約翰不是才認識沒多久？幹嘛這麼急？
海莉	嗯，我已經三十好幾了，我認為他就是對的人。
班	年紀不是問題，而且妳這麼趕一定會出事。
海莉	我是認真的！他就是我要找的人。
班	天啊，妳被愛情蒙蔽了！

EXPRESSION Guess what!

在談某件事情之前，為了吸引對方耳目的表達，「猜猜看發生什麼事」或「我跟你說一件有趣的事喔」。

Guess what! I got a job!
我跟你說！我找到工作了！

EXPRESSION What's the rush?

也可以說 What's the hurry?，意思是「幹嘛這麼急？」、「你在急什麼？」。

What's the rush? We have plenty of time!
你在急什麼？我們時間很充裕啊！

EXPRESSION in my middle 30s

表達「大約年紀」可用 in one's early（出頭）、middle（中間）、late（尾）＋ 歲數複數。

My grandmother is in her early 90s.
我奶奶九十出頭。

My mom gave a birth to me when she was in her middle 20s.
我媽在二十五歲左右生下我。

EXPRESSION Mr. Right

適合當老公的「真命天子」稱作 Mr. Right，「真命天女」稱作 Mrs. Right。

You've been with your boyfriend for a year now. Do you think he is your Mr. Right?
你現在跟男朋友交往一年了嘛，你覺得他是你的真命天子嗎？

IDIOM blinded by love

「被愛情蒙蔽雙眼」就是「情人眼裡出西施」的意思。blinded by 後面可接各種名詞，意為「被～迷惑、眼睛被遮住、看不到前面」。

Don't be blinded by money. Money can't buy happiness.
不要被錢蒙蔽雙眼，錢是買不到幸福的。

I got blinded by the sun for a second.
陽光暫時讓我看不到前面。

My gut tells me ~
我的直覺告訴我～

gut 雖然是「內臟」，但是也有「膽識」、「勇氣」或「直覺」的意思。當毫無邏輯或特別的理由，就是直覺感受到什麼的時候，就可以使用這個表達。此外，gut 的片語還有 have a gut feeling（我有個直覺）、gut reaction（本能反應）、go with my gut（順從我的直覺）等。

Mat　I'm going to invest all of my savings in a stock.

Lora　Don't put all your eggs in one basket.

Mat　I heard it from a legit source. Don't let the cat out of the bag.

Lora　💬 **My gut tells me** that this is a bad idea.

Mat　Why are you so skeptical?

Lora　Success with money requires patience and persistence. There's no way around it.

麥特　我打算梭哈我的儲蓄在一支股票上。

蘿拉　不要把你的雞蛋都擺在一個籃子裡。

麥特　我聽到一個可靠的消息，妳不要說漏嘴喔。

蘿拉　我的直覺告訴我，你這樣不 OK。

麥特　妳怎麼疑心病這麼重？

蘿拉　想賺大錢需要的是耐心和持之以恆，沒有別的捷徑。

Don't put all your eggs in one basket.

「不要把雞蛋都放在同一個籃子裡」，就是分散風險，否則失敗很可能失去一切。

**It would be wonderful if you make it as a Hollywood actor.
However, don't put all your eggs in one basket!**
如果你成為一位成功的好萊塢演員當然好啊，但是不要把雞蛋都放在同一個籃子裡。

SLANG legit

legitimate 是「合法」、「正當」、「妥當」的意思，legit 衍生為「正港」、「尚讚」、「最酷」
等意思。類似的用法還有 cool、awesome、dope 等。

Your new car is so legit!
你的新車超讚的！

Is your watch legit?
你的手錶是正牌的嗎？

IDIOM Don't let the cat out of the bag.

據說 15 世紀的英國商人會把豬裝在袋子裡賣，偶爾還會用貓來欺騙買家，因此小心別讓貓從袋子
裡跑出來，就是「別說漏嘴」、「不要洩密」的意思。

She let the cat out of the bag and spoiled the movie twist.
她暴雷，把電影的反轉說溜嘴。

EXPRESSION skeptical

「多疑」、「懷疑」的意思，可形容人的個性。相反詞是 gullible，指容易相信別人、易被騙的。
「我有點懷疑」（I'm a little skeptical.）這個說法，會比直接說「我不相信你」（I don't believe
it.）委婉，聽起來也比較有禮貌。

EXPRESSION There's no way around it.

「躲不掉」的意思，即「除了前面說到的方法外，沒其他的辦法」。

**If you want to speak English like a native, you must study a lot of idioms.
There's no way around it.**
如果你想把英文說得和母語者一樣好，一定要多學慣用語，別無他法。

It takes two to tango
一個巴掌拍不響

意為「探戈無法自己一個人跳，必須兩個人跳才行」，言下之意就是「當事情出問題，雙方都有錯和責任」，也有「想解決某事或讓某事順利進行，需要雙方共同的努力」的意思。有時候人生遇到問題時，回頭看看自己是很重要的。

Camille　I really can't trust anyone.

Toby　I know life has been rocky lately for you, but I want you to stop blaming others.

Camille　I'm trying but it is very challenging.

Toby　I'm sorry but 💬 **it takes two to tango**. You can't play the victim all the time.

Camille　I know what you mean.

Toby　It seems to me that all of your problems stem from your poor decisions.

卡蜜兒　我真的無法相信任何人。

陶比　我知道妳最近過得很辛苦，但是我希望妳不要再怪罪別人了。

卡蜜兒　我有在努力，可是好難。

陶比　我這樣說很抱歉，可是一個巴掌拍不響，妳不能總是扮演受害者。

卡蜜兒　我懂。

陶比　在我看來，妳所有的問題都源自於妳不聰明的決定。

EXPRESSION rocky

rocky「滿地石頭的」，即諸事不順遂，常用來比喻「多災多難」的意思。類似的用詞還有 rough。

She got out of her rocky marriage.
她擺脫了煎熬的婚姻生活。

I got a flat tire driving on a rocky road.
我在石頭路上開車，開到爆胎了。

EXPRESSION challenging

「具有挑戰性的」，也就是「困難，不簡單」的意思。常用的搭配詞有 challenging time（困難時期）、challenging task（有難度的任務）。challenged 是過去分詞（p.p.），常用來形容人，如 vertically challenged（身高矮的）、financially challenged（面臨財務困難的）。

It is very normal to face diversified challenges in a life journey.
人生旅途中會遇到各種難關是正常的。

EXPRESSION play the victim

扮演成受害者裝可憐，把問題和責任歸咎別人。也可以說 play the victim card。

Don't play the victim to circumstances you created.
你不要自己捅了簍子還裝可憐。

Strong people don't play the victim card but take the responsibility for their actions.
堅強的人不會裝成受害者，會為自己的行為負責。

EXPRESSION stem from~

「源自於～、由～而來」的意思。

All of humanity's problems stem from man's inability to sit quietly in a room alone.
人類的所有問題皆源自於他們無法獨自靜坐在房間裡。

——Blaise Pascal 布萊茲 • 帕斯卡

Age is just a number
年齡只是個數字

就如同字面上所表現的態度,「年齡只是個數字」這句話是在說「年紀並不重要」。類似的說法還有 <u>You are only as old as you feel.</u>,直譯的話就是「你認為自己幾歲,你就是幾歲」,表示只要心態年輕,就可以不被年齡所拘束,活得年輕。祝福各位無論到了什麼年齡,都能盡情追求夢想和願望!

Foster　Did you know there is a 55-year-old lady in my class?

Lora　For real?

Foster　Yup, she wants to be a social worker so came to college.

Lora　Wow, 💬 **age is just a number**, huh?

Foster　It is amazing how some people age like fine wine.

Lora　On the other hand, there are people who age like spoiled milk.

佛斯特　妳知道我們班上有一個 55 歲的太太嗎?

蘿拉　真的假的?

佛斯特　嗯,她想成為社會工作者,所以來念大學。

蘿拉　哇,年齡只是個數字,對吧?

佛斯特　有的人就跟紅酒一樣,越陳越香。

蘿拉　反過來說,有的人就跟牛奶一樣,放久了會發臭。

For real?

亦即 Really?「真的嗎?」的意思,是母語使用者常用的反應之一。完整的句子是 Are you for real?。類似的説法還有 Are you serious?(你是認真的嗎?);Seriously?(認真?真的假的?);Are you sure?(你確定?)等。

A: I made this chicken soup for you. 我熬了雞湯要給你喝。

B: Are you for real? OMG! Thank you! 真的假的?天啊!謝謝!

 yup

yup 是 yes(是)的口語化説法。就跟「是」可以用「嗯」、「對啊」來表示一樣,英文中也有各種口語化説法。此外還有 yep 和 yeah。

A: Are you done with your dish? 你吃完了嗎?

B: Yep! 嗯!

 Huh?

表示「嗯?」、「怎麼樣?」,放在句尾用來尋求對方肯定。類似的説法還有「Eh?」,是用於不合理、感到無法理解時的感嘆詞,表示「你在説什麼?」的意思。

It's hot, huh?
天氣很熱,對吧?

Huh? What are you talking about?
蛤?你在説什麼?

IDIOM **age like fine wine**

紅酒放得越久,味道會越來越香醇,價格也會提高,因此人們會用 age like (a) fine wine 來形容人老得優雅迷人。相反的用法則有對話提到的 age like spoiled milk,spoil 是「破壞」或是「飲食腐壞」的意思。「飲食腐壞」經常被直譯為 rot,不過母語使用者更常用 spoil 或 go bad 來表示。

George Clooney definitely aged like fine wine.
He is still hot at the age of 59.
喬治克隆尼真是越老越有魅力,59 歲了還這麼迷人。

Let's Practice!
DAY 41-50

Exercise 1　請用題目中給的單字造句。

1. 不要光從外觀來判斷事物。（judge）

_____

2. 那種行為很沒水準。（low）

_____

3. 真是個好消息。（It's music）

_____

4. 我受夠了。（sick）

_____

5. 可以改到下次嗎？（Can we take）

_____

6. 一個巴掌拍不響。（tango）

_____

7. 我的直覺告訴我你是錯的。（My guts）

_____

8. 你被愛蒙蔽了雙眼！（blind）

_____

9. 這是祕密，別說溜嘴。（cat）

_____

10. 人生難免遇到意料之外的事。（curveball）

_____

解答 1
1) Don't judge a book by its cover.
2) That's a low blow.　3) It is music to my ears.　4) I'm sick of it.　5) Can we take a rain check?
6) It takes two to tango.　7) My guts tell me that you are wrong.
8) You are blinded by love!　9) Don't let the cat out of the bag.
10) Life sometimes throws you a curveball.

依照句意填入正確答案。

1. 就是說吧！

Tell _____!

2. 我也不想這麼說。

I hate to _____.

3. 存錢以備不時之需。

Save for a _____.

4. 謝天謝地。

Thank _____.

5. 夠了！

Cut _____!

6. 不要自斷後路。

_____ bridges.

7. 會出軌的人，有第一次就有第二次。

Once a _____.

8. 年紀只是個數字。

Age is _____.

9. 欲速則不達。

Haste _____.

10. 我們得勒緊褲帶了。

_____ our belts.

解答 2
1) me about it   2) break it to you   3) rainy day   4) God   5) it out   6) Don't burn
7) cheater always a cheater   8) just a number   9) makes waste   10) We have to tighten

A blessing in disguise
因禍得福

直譯是「偽裝成壞事的祝福」，即「塞翁失馬焉知非福」，起初不幸的壞事，事後反而帶來好結果。例如遭遇挫敗後，重新站起來，反而斬獲大勝；心碎分手，卻遇到合適的終身伴侶等。類似的說法還有 Everything happens for a reason. 及 Every cloud has a silver lining.

Taylor   I think meeting John was 💬 **a blessing in disguise**.

Harry   Are you talking about your ex-husband? What makes you say that?

Taylor   Now I have an eye for good men.

Harry   No offense but you really had poor taste in men.

Taylor   True and this whole experience made me a better and bigger person.

Harry   So proud! Don't forget that I'm always rooting for you.

泰勒   我覺得遇見約翰讓我因禍得福。

哈利   妳是説妳的前夫嗎？妳為什麼會這麼想？

泰勒   現在我懂得怎麼挑男人了。

哈利   無惡意，但是妳之前真的很沒眼光。

泰勒   你説的沒錯，這段經歷幫助我成長為更好、更強大的人。

哈利   妳很棒！別忘了我永遠挺妳。

EXPRESSION **What makes you say that?**

直譯「是什麼讓你這麼說？」，表示「你為什麼會這麼想？」的意思。make 除了「製作」，也是使役動詞，「使」人做出行動，後面加原形動詞。

IDIOM **have an eye for**

如字面上的意思，指「有眼光；有能力做出正確判斷」。

You really have an eye for music.
你對音樂的品味真的很出眾。

He has a good eye for detail.
他有能力觀察到其他人忽略的細節。

EXPRESSION **No offense.**

offense 有「攻擊；進攻」的意思。如果接下來要說的話可能會冒犯到對方，常會先用 No offense. 來表示「沒有惡意」；「無意冒犯」；「我無意傷害你」。比較講究的說法有 with all due respect。

No offense to your sister but she has to get a grip.
我無意攻擊你妹妹，不過她真的該控制一下自己。

EXPRESSION **have good/bad taste in**

taste 指「味道」，也有「見解、品味」等意。可以用 have a good taste in (something) 表示眼光很好；have a bad/poor taste in (something) 則是沒眼光。

We have the same taste in men.
我們看男人的眼光一樣。

She has poor taste in fashion.
她的時尚品味很差。

TAIGLISH **「fighting」是台式英文！**

想說加油的時候，I'm rooting for you. 表示「我支持你」，意在激勵對方、給對方力量。類似的說法還有 You can do it / Go for it / hang in there! 等。

Everyone is rooting for you! Good luck tomorrow!
大家都在為你加油！祝你明天好運！

Up in the air
尚無定論

字面上的意思是「浮在空中」，意指「尚無定論」、「懸而未決」。對某件事無法作出決定，或尚在考慮該不該做某件事的時候，就可以用這句話來表示。

Sally　Got a plan for this weekend, Lora?

Lora　I was planning a little weekend getaway but everything is still  **up in the air**.

Sally　Adrienne and I are going to Vegas. Wanna join?

Lora　I'm so down.

Sally　Let's have a girl's night out!

Lora　What happens in Vegas stays in Vegas!

莎莉　蘿拉，妳週末有什麼計畫嗎？

蘿拉　我週末打算來趟小旅行，但還沒有任何確切計畫。

莎莉　亞德莉安跟我要去拉斯維加斯，妳要一起去嗎？

蘿拉　我絕對要！

莎莉　姐妹們一起大玩一場吧！

蘿拉　把發生在拉斯維加斯的事全都留在拉斯維加斯！

EXPRESSION little

可別以為 little 只有「小」的意思，little 也常用來形容「微不足道的」、「不算什麼」。

"Take off your little mask! / I want to talk to him about something little!"
「脫掉你那沒用的面具吧！/ 我想跟他小聊一下！」

——摘自小丑對蝙蝠俠說的台詞

EXPRESSION weekend getaway

getaway 當名詞代表「逃走」、「放假」。因此，weekend getaway 指的是「週末的小旅行」。
如果在網路上搜尋「weekend getaway bag」，通常會跑出適合提著走的小旅行包。

Palm spring is one of the best places for weekend getaways.
棕櫚泉是最適合週末小旅行的地方之一。

EXPRESSION Wanna join?

就跟我們說「要不要加一」時一樣，join 有「加入」、「參加」等意思。完整說法是 Do you
wanna join?，口語上常省略 Do，並把 want to 發音為 wanna。

Can I join you guys?
我可以加入你們嗎？

MOST CONFUSED I'm down!

不是我在下面，而是「我加一」表示加入。類似說法還有 I'm in. 或 I'm up for it.

I'm totally down for the movie tonight!
我舉雙手贊成今晚看電影！

CULTURE girl's night out

指女性閨蜜精心打扮，一起去夜店或氣氛不錯的地方吃喝玩樂，度過狂歡之夜。

We haven't gone on a girl's night out for a while! Let's plan it!
我們幾個姐妹很久沒晚上一起出去玩了！來約一約吧！

CULTURE What happens in Vegas stays in Vegas!

Les Vegas（拉斯維加斯）有個著名的別稱——Sin City（罪惡之城）。這裡是藥物和狂歡派對的天
堂，因此衍生出「What happens in Vegas stays in Vegas」這句話，也就是「發生在這裡的事就
跟沒發生過一樣」，不管喝得多醉、玩得多瘋、做什麼荒唐的事都可以。許多人都會從美國各地到
拉斯維加斯舉辦單身派對或生日派對徹夜狂歡，使這個地方又被稱為「The city never sleeps（不
夜城）」。

Knock out
不省人事

Knock out 有個我們更熟悉的縮寫——KO。在拳擊術語中是指選手擊倒對方，使對方無法再起。此外 knock out 在日常生活中也有累到昏睡過去的意思，形容人彷彿被擊倒般沉睡不醒。作為名詞使用時，也可以表示一個人十分迷人、有吸引力。<u>He is a knock out!</u>（我要被他帥昏了！）；<u>She is a real knock out!</u>（她真的正到我發瘋！）

James	I couldn't get ahold of you last night. What happened?
Lora	I was  **knocked out** as soon as I got home.
James	I thought you were ghosting me.
Lora	Oh, give me a break!
James	Well, you left me on read too!
Lora	Better than sleep texting like last time!

詹姆士	昨晚怎麼聯絡不上妳？
蘿拉	我回家就睡死了。
詹姆士	我以為妳在搞消失。
蘿拉	吼，放過我吧。
詹姆士	而且妳還已讀我。
蘿拉	至少沒有像上次一樣在半夢半醒之間亂傳訊息！

get ahold of (someone)

跟字面上一樣有「抓著某人不放」的意思，不過也可以用來表示「跟某人取得聯絡」。

I got ahold of jenny.
我聯絡上珍妮了。

 「搞失蹤」正確的英文怎麼說？

ghost 是「鬼」的意思，鬼跟沒有回應的朋友的共通點是「不見蹤影」，所以「不理某人」的英文就是 ghost somebody。

I got ghosted by my ex-boyfriend.
我前男友跟我搞消失。

I don't understand why people ghost out of the blue.
我不懂為什麼有些人會突然搞消失。

 Give me a break!

當一個人說「讓我休息」，就是在告訴對方「別逼我」、「夠了」、「適可而止」等意思。此外，也可以用這句話表示不相信對方所說的話。

Mom: Are you done cleaning your room?
媽媽：妳整理好房間了沒？

Daughter: Oh, Mom! Give me a break! I'm on it!
女兒：吼唷！媽！不要唸了！我在收了！

 「已讀不回」正確的英文怎麼說？

left on read 是「被已讀不回」，而傳訊息「不讀不回」則是 left unread。

Better left unread than dead. Don't text and drive.
不讀不回總比沒命好，不要邊開車邊傳訊息。

 sleep texting

指半夢半醒間傳訊息，隔天醒來卻想不起來的行為。大部分用來形容像夢話般沒頭沒腦的訊息或是牛頭不對馬嘴的回覆。

You took the words right out of my mouth
那正是我想說的話

「把我想說的話從我的口中拿出來」，當對方先說出了自己原本想說的話時，就可以用這句話來表達「那正是我要說的」。另外，也可以解釋為「我就是那個意思」，表示完全贊同。類似的說法還有 I was just about to say that.

Aran   You look gorgeous in every photo!

Lora   💬 **You took the words right out of my mouth!**
You pull off every style so perfectly.

Aran   How do you manage your time to do everything you do?

Lora   That's been my question for you! You inspire me in every way.

Aran   Thank you for saying that.

Lora   I would like to follow in your footsteps.

艾倫   妳每張照片都很好看！

蘿拉   妳搶了我的台詞！妳每種風格都消化得很好。

艾倫   妳是怎麼安排時間，把每件事都做好的？

蘿拉   我才想問妳咧！妳總是帶給我很多啟發。

艾倫   謝謝妳這麼說。

蘿拉   我很想向妳學習。

EXPRESSION gorgeous

母語者常用意指「十分動人」、「美麗」，程度上比 beautiful 更讚嘆。其他相似詞還有 fabulous、fantastic、stunning、excellent、perfect 等。

Newport Beach is gorgeous!
紐波特比奇真的太美了！

EXPRESSION pull off

表示「為了靠邊停車，把車駛離車道」；「下高速公路」；「拔掉」；「搞定困難的事」；「促成某事」；「駕馭」等各種不同的意思。

Pull off the highway at Culver.
在卡爾弗城下高速公路。

I pulled off the road because I think I'm lost.
我覺得我迷路了，所以把車開到路邊停了下來。

Congrats! You pulled off a million-dollar deal!
恭喜！你促成了 100 萬美金的交易！

EXPRESSION in every way

指「各方面」、「各種層面」。別忘了！ every 後面必須接單數名詞，不能用複數名詞。

We are getting better in every way as we get old. 隨著年齡增長，我們的各方面都在進步。	**I will help you in every way possible.** 我會盡可能在各種層面幫助你。

IDIOM follow in one's footsteps

footsteps 是「腳步」，有足跡的意思，也可以用來比喻過去的經歷。「循著某人的腳步前進」表示「追隨敬仰的對象或家人」。

I don't want my son to follow in my footsteps and be a doctor. I just want him to be happy.
我不希望我的兒子追隨我的腳步成為一位醫生。我只希望他開心就好。

I want to follow in Jesus's footsteps by loving others.
我想要效法耶穌愛人如己的精神。

on the tip of my tongue
好像就快想起來了

「話在舌尖」，也就是話都到了嘴邊卻想不起來怎麼說，表示「就快想起來了」。一時之間想不起電影名稱、人名，就可以說這句話。也可以用於「欲言又止」，話說到一半，卻選擇吞下去不說出口。

Sam	I ran across one of your friends the other day.
Lora	Who?
Sam	Her name is 💬 **on the tip of my tongue**. She works for whatchamacallit....
Lora	Anna? Sarah?
Sam	Argh, I can't think of her name off the top of my head.
Lora	It's OK. It happens all the time.

山姆	我不久前碰到了妳的朋友。
蘿拉	誰？
山姆	我一時之間想不起名字。那個，她在那邊工作……
蘿拉	安娜？莎拉？
山姆	啊，想不起來叫什麼名字。
蘿拉	沒關係，想不起來很正常。

EXPRESSION run across

「偶然遇見」、「偶然發現」。也可以照字面上的意思當作「穿越道路」。類似的說法還有 run into / bump into / come across。

Run across the street and you will see me.
你過馬路就會看到我了。

I ran across a 100-dollar bill and I was thrilled but decided to report it.
我撿到了一百美金，雖然很開心，但我決定交給警察。

SPOKEN ENGLISH whatchamacallit

「那叫什麼？」；「那個怎麼說？」口語化的說法，把 What you may call it? 唸快一點，合成一個單字，就會是 whatchamacallit。這個字通常會在想不起來某人或某物的名稱時以自言自語的方式出現，如果沒聽說過這種說法的話，乍聽之下可能聽不出來是英文，而不知該如何反應。類似的說法有 What do you call it?

A: Could you hand me, that... you know, whatchamacallit. Um...
可以幫我拿一下那個，呃，那叫什麼，嗯……

B: Hand you what?
幫你拿什麼？

EXCLAMATION argh

「啊」、「呃啊」的感嘆詞，用於表示煩躁、生氣、恐懼的情緒。類似的說法有 ugh。

Argh! This is so aggravating!
啊！這真的讓人很不爽！

Ugh, I'm so sick of this.
呃，我真的快受不了了。

IDIOM off the top of my head

不花太多時間思考，即時反應出想法或點子。如果碰到如本文，一時之間想不起來，就可以否定形式使用這個片語。

I don't exactly know off the top of my head.
我一時之間想不到答案。

Off the top of my head, I think about 10 people are coming.
我猜大概會來 10 個人左右。

Day 56

On a power trip
耍大牌、仗勢欺人

形容人自認為高人一等,做出壓迫、霸凌他人的行為。利用自己的權力做出
非法或不道德的行為,則可以用 abuse one's power(濫用權力)。不論處
於何種社經地位,人人都應該受到尊重、平等對待。

Christina It is obnoxious how Jenny bosses us around
these days.

James She has changed after making it as an
influencer on Instagram.

Christina I think she is 💬 **on a power trip**.

James I'm happy for her but we have no reason to
be treated this way.

Christina We should talk it out. Let her know how we
feel.

James Yeah, we should.

克莉絲汀娜 珍妮最近老是對我們頤指氣使,真的很討厭。

詹姆士 她自從在 Instagram 上變網紅後就變了一個人。

克莉絲汀娜 我看她就是在耍大牌。

詹姆士 看到她發展得不錯我很開心,可是我們沒理由接受這種
待遇。

克莉絲汀娜 我們應該跟她談一談,讓她知道我們的感受。

詹姆士 嗯,的確要。

EXPRESSION **obnoxious**

obnoxious 意為「令人不快的」、「粗魯無禮的」。想要表達「荒謬讓人無言」時可以用 ridiculous、absurd 等，而不爽到無言以對則用 obnoxious。

I can't stand his obnoxious behavior.
他的行為實在可惡到讓人説不出話來，我受不了。

IDIOM **boss (someone) around**

把自己當成 boss（上司）使喚他人的行為就叫做 boss around。當然，這句話也有字面上的含義，表示居上位者下達指示。

Don't boss me around!
不要使喚我！

Ken bosses his employees around as a person in charge.
肯以負責人的身分對他的員工下指示。

TAIGLISH **「網紅」英文怎麼説？**

台灣人經常喜歡説 KOL (Key Opinion Leader)「意見領袖」，其實外國人可能聽得霧煞煞。正確的説法應該是 influencer，透過社群媒體「有影響力的人」。

EXPRESSION **I'm happy for (someone).**

這句話常拿來表達賀意，聽説其他人有好消息的時候這麼説，就能傳達出看到你幸福我也很開心的意思，可以解釋為「真好」；「真棒」；「太好了」。也可以替換成其他形容詞，表達不同心情。

A: I finally passed the exam! 我終於考過了！

B: Congrats! I'm so happy for you! 恭喜！真是太好了！

I'm truly excited for Anna that she found her better half.
看到安娜找到她的另一半，我真的很為她開心。

I'm sad for you. 我為你感到難過。

EXPRESSION **talk it out**

out 有「往外」的含義，所以 talk it out 就表示坦白説出心裡話。根據上下文的不同，也有把話説開，解開心結的意思。

We talked it out. We are okay now.
我們把話説開，現在沒事了。

Bend over backwards
竭盡全力

可以照字面上的意思表示「向後彎腰」，也可以用來比喻為了達成某事「竭盡全力」。向後彎腰這個動作光用想的就覺得挺困難的吧？想維持這個動作絕對不是件省力的事。這個片語尤其常用來形容為了幫助他人鞠躬盡瘁或是費盡心思讓他人開心的情形。

Casey	Kevin, the newbie, seems like a total suck-up.
Dan	He really 💬 **bends over backwards** to please everyone.
Casey	Exactly!
Dan	But in a way I also think he could just be a nice guy by nature.
Casey	Well, I think he is a total people pleaser.
Dan	Let's not be so quick to judge. After all we don't really know him.

凱西	新來的凱文看起來好像是個馬屁精。
丹	他真的想盡辦法想討好大家。
凱西	就是說啊！
丹	不過從另個角度來說，我也覺得他可能本來人就這麼好。
凱西	嗯，他在我眼裡完全就是在討好別人。
丹	別太快下定論，說到底我們並不了解他。

SLANG **newbie**

這個字跟 noob（小白、菜鳥）一樣指網路遊戲經驗值不足的人，有負面的意涵。不過根據情況或上下文的不同，也可以拿來指稱「新生」、「新進員工」、「剛接觸新領域的初學者」。

I'm a freshman. I'm a newbie!
我是大一新生！

SLANG **suck-up**

指為了獲得利益，或為了討好他人「阿諛奉承的人」，當名詞或動詞使用都可以。類似的説法還有比較粗俗的 ass-kisser。

I can't stand those suck-ups on our team.
我受不了我們組裡那些馬屁精。

Stop sucking up to your professor to get an A.
不要再為了拿好成績奉承教授了。

EXPRESSION **by nature**

「自然地」，也就是「本來」、「天生的」、「天性使然」的意思。

She is not an evil person by nature. She is conditioned by her environment.
她本性不壞，只是環境使然。

EXPRESSION **people pleaser**

「討好他人者」，也就是比起自己的感受更在意他人的眼光，「迎合他人喜好的人」，這樣的人通常不善於拒絕，容易被牽著鼻子走。

Don't be a people pleaser. You can't please everyone. Just be yourself.
不要一味討好他人，你不可能滿足所有人，做自己就好。

EXPRESSION **after all**

這個片語很難直譯理解，意思是（與料想不同）「結果」、「終究」、「總之」、「畢竟」。也可以加在句首、句尾，強調所述內容是事實。

We won the game after all. Who would've known?
結果是我們贏了比賽，誰能料得到呢？

I love you after all.
終究我還是愛你的。

Sweep under the rug
掩蓋問題

「用掃把把灰塵掃到地毯下藏起來」，這句片語是把羞恥或有礙顏面的壞事當作秘密隱瞞起來的意思，也指對問題視若無睹，逃避面對。類似的說法還有 sweep under the carpet。

Camille   Taylor lost it the other day.

Henry   It is my 3rd time seeing her having a mental breakdown.

Camille   Her problem with her husband seems like an elephant in the room, but can we all talk about it?

Henry   It just can't be 💬 **swept under the rug** like this.

Camille   She talks about getting a divorce and 5 min later plans a family trip.

Henry   I know. We are all confused.

卡蜜兒   泰勒前幾天失控了。

亨利   這已經是我第三次目睹她崩潰了。

卡蜜兒   她跟老公間的問題眾所皆知，卻沒人敢談，我們一起談一談如何？

亨利   不能再逃避這個問題了。

卡蜜兒   她才說要離婚，五分鐘後又開始計劃家庭旅行。

亨利   就是說啊，我們都很不解。

EXPRESSION lose it

lose 有「失去」的意思，lose it 代表「失去理智地發怒或哭泣、大笑」。

I lost it when he left me.
他離開我的時候我崩潰了。

I don't remember last night. I just lost it and went crazy.
我不記得昨晚發生了什麼事，我整個人ㄅㄧㄤ掉了。

MOST CONFUSED 3rd time

「第三次」的英文需要使用「序數」，第一 first（1st）、第二 second（2nd）、第三 third（3rd）、第四 fourth（4th）、第五 fifth（5th）……數字後加 th。注意 twenty、thirty 要去 y 加 ieth，第二十 twentieth（20th）、第三十 thirtieth（30th）；第二十一 twenty first（21st）。

Halloween falls on 31st of October.
萬聖節在 10 月 31 日。

MOST ASKED 「精神崩潰」正確的英文怎麼說？

正是「mental（精神）breakdown（崩潰）」。也涵蓋因精神負擔太重導致無法正常生活，罹患恐慌症或是憂鬱症等情形。我們所說的「精神崩潰」可以適用於比較輕鬆、玩笑的語氣，英文裡的 mental breakdown 語感上則比較沈重嚴肅。類似的表達方式還有 nervous breakdown。

Because I had a mental breakdown I cried and screamed for hours.
由於精神崩潰，我哭喊了幾個小時。

I suffered a nervous breakdown last year. I barely slept, went out and talked.
我去年遇到神經衰弱的問題，幾乎無法入眠，也不太出門或開口說話。

IDIOM an elephant in the room

如果房間裡有一隻大象，房裡的人不可能不去注意到牠的存在。這個片語正是用來比喻面對重大且顯而易見的問題，對其避而不談、視而不見的現象。

Taylor being the victim of domestic violence is an elephant in the room. She just wants to sweep it under the rug.
泰勒是家暴受害者，茲事體大，卻隱藏在心裡。她只想逃避這個問題。

I saw it coming
我早就預料到

原句是 <u>I saw it coming a mile away.</u>，常省略 a mile away。表示「早就預料會發生，並不意外」。語氣上可以是正面也可以是負面的，例如 I didn't see it coming.（我沒想到會這樣。）；I should have seen it coming.（我早該要預料到會發生這種事才對。）等，可以活用於日常生活中的各種狀況。

Jackson Have you seen the news about Irene, the K-POP star?

Lora It came as no surprise. 💬 **I kind of saw it coming.**

Jackson Give me the inside scoop! You are in the industry.

Lora I would rather not say.

Jackson You can't just brush over it like that. I want details!

Lora Since I didn't see it with my own eyes I shouldn't be talking about it.

傑克森 妳有看到那個韓星 Irene 的新聞嗎？
蘿拉 我不意外，我本來就有點預感。
傑克森 跟我分享一下妳的專業見解！畢竟妳在那個圈子工作。
蘿拉 還是別多說比較好。
傑克森 別想輕輕帶過，我要聽細節！
蘿拉 畢竟不是我親眼所見，我不該多嘴。

EXPRESSION **It came as no surprise.**

表示「對於某件事會發生並不感到驚訝」。跟 I saw it coming. 的意思相近。

Their divorce came as no surprise.
他們的離婚並不令人意外。

EXPRESSION **the inside scoop**

只有內部人員或親友才知道的消息。scoop 可以指一勺的量、挖冰淇淋的動作或「勺子」，也有「獨家新聞」的意思。

Since she is everyone's best friend she always has the inside scoop.
她跟所有人都很要好，所以知道各種獨家消息。

Can I have a single scoop of chocolate?
麻煩給我一球巧克力冰淇淋。

IDIOM **brush over**

有「刷上顏色」的意思，不過也指「對某事輕描淡寫」。草草帶過或跳過某個話題，只提到粗淺資訊，也有「不在意、忽略、敷衍」的含義。

You can't just brush over the fact why you couldn't make it to my birthday party.
你要說清楚為什麼不能來我的生日派對，別想草草帶過。

Let's just brush over the result and move on to the next subject.
我們大致梳理一下結論，然後進入下一個主題吧。

EXPRESSION **see (something) with one's own eyes**

如字面意思，「親眼看到」。親耳聽到則是 hear (something) with one's own ears。這兩個片語常用於對某些事物感到難以置信的情況，如同本文中的用法，以否定句呈現。也可以反過來以肯定句強調是自己的見聞來證明某事。

I don't believe anything before I see it with my own eyes.
除非是我親眼所見，不然我不會輕易相信任何事。

Count your blessings
想想你有多幸福

blessing 是「祝福」的意思。bless（祝福）是美國文化中很重要的元素。美國總統的演說經常以「God bless America!」作結尾。如果有人打噴嚏，就算是陌生人也會對打噴嚏的人說「Bless you!」作為禮貌問候。不只是難熬或絕望，平時也要珍惜所擁有的事物，心懷感激，正是 Count your blessings. 的含義。此刻我們活在同一片天空下，這本身就是一件值得感恩的事。

Jess	What have you been up to lately?
Brandy	I've hit rock bottom and I'm trying to survive.
Jess	I'm so sorry. I had no idea.
Brandy	I've been physically and mentally drained.
Jess	Please remember that you are never alone. Reach out and we are here.
Brandy	Thank you. I'm just trying to 💬 **count my blessings**.

潔絲	妳最近在做什麼？
布蘭迪	我遇到了低潮，正在努力擺脫。
潔絲	我很遺憾，我完全不知道妳的狀況。
布蘭迪	我的身體跟精神都很疲憊。
潔絲	別忘了妳不是一個人，我們都在妳身邊。
布蘭迪	謝謝，我會試著提醒自己我已經很幸福了。

EXPRESSION What have you been up to?

What are you up to? 是母語使用者常用來表示「在做什麼？」或「在忙什麼？」的問候語。如果使用現在完成式 What have you been up to? 就是在問「近來你過得怎麼樣？」下次除了 How are you? / What's up? 之外，也試著用母語使用者常用的説法做變化吧。

What are you up to right now? Wanna hang out?
你現在在幹嘛？要不要出來玩？

MOST MISTAKEN lately

lately 意指「近來」、「不久前」。很多台灣人經常搞混，把 lately 當成 late 的副詞型態。late（遲的、晚的）的副詞型態還是 late，不變。

I slept late last night.
I slept lately. (×)
我昨天很晚睡。

I haven't been sleeping enough lately.
我最近睡眠不足。

IDIOM hit rock bottom

就如字面上的意思，rock bottom 意謂著「石頭底部」。這個片語的意思是「跌到谷底」，指陷入最糟的狀況，不會再更差了。也指某物掉落到最底部。

Stock market hit rock bottom due to the pandemic.
疫情導致股市跌到谷底。

EXPRESSION drained

指「把水等物體排出」，也用來比喻「力氣、精神耗盡」。

I always feel so drained after meeting new people.
認識新朋友總讓我覺得精疲力盡。

IDIOM reach out

就如字面上所描述，這個片語表示「伸出手」，也有「取得聯繫」的意思，大部分用於向他人請求協助的情況。不過也要記得，它還有「伸出援手」的意思！

We all need to reach out to people in need.
我們都應該向需要的人伸出援手。

Let's Practice!
DAY 51-60

Exercise 1 請用題目中給的單字造句。

1. 我早就預料到了。（I saw）

_____

2. 我陷入了低潮。（I've hit）

_____

3. 我以為你在對我搞消失。（I thought）

_____

4. 我們把話説開吧。（talk）

_____

5. 你能駕馭所有造型。（pull）

_____

6. 我睡死了。（knock）

_____

7. 泰勒失去了理智。（lose）

_____

8. 我加入！（I'm）

_____

9. 那正是我要説的！（You took）

_____

10. 加油！（root）

_____

解答 1

1) I saw it coming.   2) I've hit rock bottom.   3) I thought you were ghosting me.   4) Let's talk it out.   5) You pull off every style.   6) I was knocked out.   7) Taylor lost it.   8) I'm down!
9) You took the words right out of my mouth!   10) I'm rooting for you!

Exercise 2 依照句意填入正確答案。

1. 那叫什麼來著。

W_____.

2. 迎合他人喜好者

People _____

3. 因禍得福

A blessing _____

4. 伸出援手

_____ out

5. 竭盡全力

_____ backwards

6. 仗勢欺人

On _____

7. 想想你有多幸福吧。

Count _____.

8. 還不確定。

It's up _____.

9. 掩蓋、隱瞞問題

Sweep _____

10. 一時之間想不起來。

It's on the tip of _____.

解答 2
1) Whatchamacallit   2) pleaser   3) in disguise   4) Reach   5) Bend over
6) a power trip   7) your blessings   8) in the air   9) under the rug   10) my tongue

You look young for your age
就你的年紀來說，你看起來很年輕

表示「看起來比實際年齡年輕」。想要稱讚人外貌保養得當的時候是十分實用的說法，不過對實際年紀還很年輕的人說這句話，對方可能會產生「難道我應該要看起來比較老嗎？」的誤會。類似的表達方式還有 You look great for your age. 或 You don't look your age. 等。

Taylor   Lora, this is John. John, this is Lora.

Lora   Pleasure meeting you. I've heard a lot about you.

John   Nice to meet you. Wow, 💬 **you look young for your age**!

Lora   Thank you! You've just made my day.

John   I heard you are a social butterfly.

Lora   Yes, I'm a bit of a people person.

泰勒   蘿拉，這是約翰。約翰，這是蘿拉。

蘿拉   很高興認識你，我常聽泰勒提到你。

約翰   很高興認識妳。哇，妳看來比實際年紀年輕很多！

蘿拉   謝謝！有你這句話我可以開心一整天。

約翰   聽說妳朋友很多。

蘿拉   是，我喜歡與人交流。

MOST MISTAKEN This is ~.

用英文介紹朋友認識時，很常誤用成 She/He is~。就像中文介紹人時說「這位是～」語氣比較有禮，英文要用 This is~ 才對。接電話時也不能說 I'm Lora.，應該說 This is Lora.（我是蘿拉）才是正確的表達方式。

Hello, this is Lora speaking. How may I help you?
喂？我是蘿拉，有什麼需要我幫忙的嗎？

EXPRESSION You made my day.

「你創造了我的一天」，意思是「你讓我今天心情很美好」。下次有人稱讚，或做出讓你開心的舉動時，就可以說 You made my day. 代替 Thank you!。在社群媒體看到有趣的貼文，網友也經常留言這句話的縮寫 YMMD（這篇貼文讓我笑死了）。

Thank you for coffee. I need it. You've made my day!
謝謝你的咖啡，我正需要來一杯。你讓今天美好了起來！

Those beautiful flowers from my boyfriend totally made my day yesterday.
我男友昨天送我的花讓我開心了一整天。

EXPRESSION social butterfly

形容一個人個性友善、善於社交、交友廣泛，可以與各種不同個性的人相處融洽。也可以用 popular（受歡迎）來代替。

Bob is a social butterfly. He gets along with everyone.
鮑伯是個社交高手，他跟每個人都處得來。

EXPRESSION people person

people person 是指「喜歡與人相處的人」。可以在 person 前加上各種名詞來表示「喜歡～的人」。

Are you a cat person or a dog person?
你是貓派還是狗派？

I'm not a beer person. I'm more of a wine person.
我沒那麼喜歡啤酒，我更喜歡紅酒。

Drink like a fish
牛飲、豪飲

用魚在水中嘴巴一張一合喝水的樣子來形容大口喝酒的動作，表示喝很多酒的意思。這個片語可以用來描述某人習慣性地經常飲酒，有時具有負面意義，不過也可以單純指某天偶然喝得特別多。多數情況指喝酒，亦適用於水或其他飲料。

Kyle 💬 **I drank like a fish** last night and I'm dying.

Lora You must have a horrible hangover. How much did you drink?

Kyle Not much actually. I'm a cheap drunk so I usually don't drink.

Lora Really? I thought you are a heavy drinker.

Kyle I get that a lot. I'm just a social drinker.

Lora Now I know. Let's go nurse your hangover!

凱爾 我昨天飲酒過量，快死了。

蘿拉 你宿醉一定很嚴重吧。你喝了多少？

凱爾 其實沒有很多，只是我酒量很差，所以不常喝。

蘿拉 真的嗎？我以為你是個酒鬼。

凱爾 很多人都這麼說，不過我只會為了社交多少喝一點。

蘿拉 了解。我們來想辦法解決你的宿醉吧！

EXPRESSION I'm dying~

就如本文所示，這個片語是指因為飢餓、疼痛、生氣、被工作纏身等各種狀況導致難過得「快死了」的意思。不過用於 <I'm dying + to 不定詞 > 或 <I'm dying for + 名詞 > 時，則有「想做某事想得快死了」或「瘋狂地想要某個東西」的意思。

I'm dying to see you.
我想你想得快死了。

I'm dying for a Porsche.
我想要一台保時捷想得快瘋了。

EXPRESSION cheap drunk

cheap 除了是「廉價的」，也有「不費力氣，易得到的」。cheap drunk 指喝一點酒就會醉的人。

EXPRESSION I get that a lot.

「我常得到那樣的話」，表示「我常聽人那麼跟我說」。

A: Wow, you have beautiful eyes! 哇，你的眼睛很漂亮！

B: I get that a lot. 很多人都這麼說。

EXPRESSION social drinker

「社交飲酒者」，只會在特殊日子或社交場合才小酌的人。類似的用法還有 social smoker，指平時不抽菸，僅在聊天交際時抽菸的人。

EXPRESSION nurse one's hangover

hangover 意指「宿醉」。中文會說解宿醉，但英文則是「照護」、「治療」宿醉，所以這裡的動詞是 nurse 或 cure。

I eat a burger or drink milk to nurse my hangover.
我通常會吃漢堡或喝牛奶來緩解宿醉。

How do you usually nurse your hangover?
你通常怎麼解決宿醉問題？

Getting plenty of sleep is the best hangover cure.
睡飽就是解決宿醉最好的辦法。

I'm all ears
我洗耳恭聽

全身都是耳朵？這句慣用語是指「非常專心地側耳傾聽」，或「準備好要洗耳恭聽」。也有告訴對方「我有在聽，別擔心」的意思。語意可能依據情況或上下文的不同而略有差異。其他類似的身體部位慣用語還有：be all eyes 目不轉睛；注意地看。be all heart 全心全意；心地善良。be all mouth 整天出一張嘴；只說不做。

Boss　Jill, are you following me?

Jill　Yes, 💬 **I'm all ears**, sir.

Boss　Recap what I've just said.

Jill　Sorry, I zoned out for a sec.

Boss　Let's call it a day. I'm a bit tired too.

Jill　(I'm so doomed...)

上司　吉兒，妳有跟上我的節奏嗎？

吉兒　是，我有在聽。

上司　那妳歸納一下我剛剛說的話。

吉兒　抱歉，我剛剛有點恍神。

上司　今天就到這裡吧，我也有點累了。

吉兒　（我完了……）

EXPRESSION Are you following me?

可以照字面上的意思表示「你有跟著我嗎？」，不過也有「你有聽懂我說的話嗎？」的意思。

Wait, I'm not following you.
等等，我不太懂你的意思。

EXPRESSION recap

recapitulate 的簡寫，意指「概括」、「歸納」。意味著從整體內容摘取出重點，也有「回顧、複習」的意思。

Let's briefly recap on the last meeting we had.
來簡單統整一下上次會議的重點吧。

Watch a recap on season 2 before starting season 3.
在看第三季之前，先來回顧第二季的回顧吧。

IDIOM zone out

有「睡著」、「失去意識」、「恍神」等含義，不過最常用於表示「發呆」。類似的說法還有 space out（放空）。

Hey! You can't zone out on me.
喂！你不要在我說話的時候放空。

I just zone out when he talks.
只要他一講話我就會恍神。

IDIOM call it a day

事情做得差不多或想要休息的時候，就可以用這句話來表示到此為止。有「工作結束」、「收工」、「到此為止」等含義。類似的表達方式還有 call it a night，但這句話適用於停止手上的工作，去睡覺或結束一整天的情況。

I'm going to call it a night and go to bed early.

I have a big day ahead of me.
我要早點收工去睡覺了，明天是個大日子。

EXPRESSION doomed

意謂「被詛咒的」、「不幸的」，用來表示「糟糕了」、「死定了」，有「注定沒有好結果或失敗收場」等各種含義，日常生活中經常如本文所示用以比喻「完蛋了」。

Every Jack has his Jill

姻緣天注定，有一天會找到對象。

〈Jack and Jill〉是一首有名的英文童謠，以常見的男女名字泛指平凡男女。「所有的 Jack 都會遇見自己的 Jill」，也就是「不管是怎樣的男人，這世界上一定都有適合他的伴侶」的意思。也可以反過來以「Every Jill has her own Jack.」來表示「每個女人一定都有適合她的另一半」。

Naomi	Are you still seeing that girl?
Henry	I'm sorta but I don't know if she is playing hard to get or just not interested.
Naomi	Well, don't let her play with your heart.
Henry	I know but I like how she is not clingy and needy.
Naomi	Your ex was way too obsessive and possessive.
Henry	People say **every Jack has his Jill**! I'm sure there is someone out there for me.

娜歐米	你還有跟那個女生曖昧嗎？
亨利	算吧，但我不知道她是在對我欲擒故縱還是對我沒興趣。
娜歐米	唔，你可別被她玩弄了。
亨利	我知道，但我喜歡她不黏人、不需要過度關懷。
娜歐米	你的前女友實在太執著、佔有慾太強了。
亨利	大家都說姻緣天注定！我相信這世界一定有我的另一半。

EXPRESSION **seeing**

動詞 see 可不是只有「看」的意思，也可以表示「與誰交往」。但因為愛情觀因人而異，see 也可以指還在瞭解對方，彼此約會曖昧。

How long have you been seeing each other?
你們交往多久了？

I don't have a girlfriend but sorta seeing a few girls.
我沒有女朋友，但有認識一些女生。

SPOKEN ENGLISH **sorta**

sort of 的口語化說法，就跟 kind of 可以縮略為 kinda 或 kina 一樣。有「某種程度上」、「多少」、「有點」、「某種的」等意思，在不知該說什麼的時候也能用來表示「該怎麼說呢」。sorta 亦可與 kinda 合起來一起使用。

I'm sorta tired. I don't think I will go out tonight.
我有點累，今晚應該不會出門。

I kinda sorta like Jay.
我有點喜歡杰伊。

MOST ASKED **戀愛中的「欲擒故縱」正確的英文怎麼說？**

為了吸引對方的關注並讓對方看到自己的魅力，而故作冷漠、沒有興趣，用英文來描述這種欲擒故縱的行為就是 play hard to get。

I don't like to play hard to get.
我不喜歡欲擒故縱。

EXPRESSION **clingy and needy**

clingy 指的是每分每秒都不願意分開，只想黏在一起的「黏人」，經常與 needy 連用。needy 是 need（需要）的形容詞，意謂著需要大量且不間斷的愛和關懷。渴望愛情又難以被滿足的狀態就可以用 needy 來表示。

Babies are usually extremely clingy.
小嬰兒通常非常黏人。

EXPRESSION **obsessive and possessive**

clingy and needy 還算可愛，obsessive and possessive 程度上就比較嚴重了，意謂著「執著、想佔有」。這兩個詞也一樣經常連在一起使用。雖然與 clingy and needy 相似，但別忘了它們之間的程度差異。

Jack was obsessive and possessive.
He made me delete all the guys from Facebook.
傑克太執著、佔有慾太強了。 他逼我把臉書上的男性朋友全都刪掉。

I'm not cut out for it
我不是那塊料

意指「我不適合某事」，形容對某事「沒有天分」。也可以用於表示能力不足，天性上不適合在特定領域活動或執行某項工作的情況，表示「這不是我該做的事」或「我做不到」。反之，也可以用 I'm cut out for it. 來表達「我適合這項工作；我對某件事有天賦」。

Taylor	Hateful comments on my YouTube really get under my skin.
Joseph	Don't let it get to you! It's inevitable.
Taylor	I think 💬 **I'm not cut out for this**. Everything is too overwhelming these days.
Joseph	Do not respond to those nasty comments.
Taylor	Hate only begets hate.
Joseph	Exactly. Embrace differences and just let them be.

泰勒	我的 YouTube 頻道上好多惡意留言，好煩。
喬瑟夫	妳別把那些留言放在心上！那是難免的。
泰勒	我覺得我不適合這一行。這一切對我來說太難承受了。
喬瑟夫	別理那些酸民留言。
泰勒	仇恨只會招致更多仇恨。
喬瑟夫	對，一樣米養百樣人，妳必須接受這個事實。

「酸民留言」的英文是？

「留言」的英文是 comment，酸民留言就是指「惡意留言」hateful comments，也可以使用 nasty comments。散發留言的「酸民」稱為 troll。這種「網路霸凌」的行為稱為 cyber bullying。

Hateful comments are like poison!
酸民留言就像毒藥一樣！

 get under one's skin

被某種東西鑽進皮膚底下的感覺一定很不舒服吧，這個片語就是指「激起煩躁和憤怒的感覺」。也有「對某人的了解十分深入」；「越來越好」；「帶來正面影響」；「經常想起某人、執著於某人，彷彿刻在皮膚裡一樣」等各種含義，可以活用於不同的狀況。

My husband of 40 years has gotten under my skin.
我跟我丈夫結縭 40 年，他對我的了解已經深入骨子裡了。

The fact that my rival had gotten a better score really got under my skin.
我的對手拿到的分數比我高，這讓我很不爽。

I only saw her once but she has gotten under my skin.
I can't stop thinking about her.
我只見過她一次，但她的樣子已經刻在我的心裡。我一直在想她。

EXPRESSION inevitable

有「無法避免的」、「必然的」或是「意料之中的」等含義，形容某件事物無人能抵擋或躲避得了。

Death is inevitable.
人終將一死。

Economic crisis seems inevitable due to the COVID-19 pandemic.
由於 COVID-19 的肆虐，經濟危機似乎是不可避免的。

EXPRESSION overwhelming

意指「壓倒性的」、「過於強烈的」。用於表現負面含義時可解釋為「負擔過重」，正面含義則有「令人興奮」、「令人激動」等意思，依據前後文及情況的不同可能出現完全相反的詞義。

Workload here is way too overwhelming for me to handle.
這裡的工作量大到我難以承受。

Just around the corner!
即將來臨！

這句話給人一種轉個彎就會看到的感覺，表示「就快到了」、「近在眼前」。常見的用法有 Christmas is just around the corner!（聖誕節就快到了！）；Prosperity is just around the corner.（成功指日可待。）等。不過如果有人說 I live just around the corner. 那就真的是在形容他的家很近，拐個彎就會到。

Sister	Christmas is 💬 **just around the corner**!
Brother	It is my favorite time of the year.
Sister	I'm gonna wait underneath the mistletoe for my Prince Charming. Haha!
Brother	Good luck. Let's hang stockings upon the fireplace tonight!
Sister	Woo, why don't we go shopping for gingerbread cookies and candy canes now?
Brother	Right on!

姐姐	馬上就是聖誕節了！
弟弟	一年之中我最喜歡這個時候了。
姐姐	我要在檞寄生下等我的白馬王子出現，哈哈！
弟弟	祝妳好運。我們今晚來把襪子掛在壁爐上吧！
姐姐	噢，我們何不現在去買薑餅跟拐杖糖？
弟弟	好啊！

CULTURE It's my favorite time of the year.

每到聖誕季總是能聽到人們把這句話掛在嘴邊。美國人一年中最重要、最盛大的節日就是聖誕節。歌手安迪威廉斯（Andy Williams）有一首聖誕歌曲〈It's the Most Wonderful Time of the Year〉，光看歌名就能感受到人們對聖誕節的喜愛。當美國人說這句話時，通常指的就是聖誕假期。

CULTURE underneath the mistletoe

mistletoe 是植物「槲寄生」，美國人相信只要在 mistletoe 下接吻，愛情就會實現。大家有注意到嗎？每年聖誕節都會風靡全球一次的聖誕歌曲 —— 瑪麗亞凱莉的〈All I Want for Christmas Is You〉，歌詞中也有寫到「I'm just gonna keep on waiting underneath the mistletoe」。也推薦另一首聖誕歌曲，年輕人的偶像小賈斯汀的〈Mistletoe〉，第一句就是前面學過的「It's the most beautiful time of the year」哦。

MOST MISTAKEN stockings

stocking 指長至膝蓋以上的長筒襪。每逢聖誕節掛在牆上或壁爐上的襪子就叫做 Christmas stocking。不過要小心，若是女用包覆到腰部的「褲襪」，正確的英文是 pantyhose、hosiery。而 leggings 則是「運動緊身褲」。

CULTURE gingerbread cookies

大家記得動畫電影《史瑞克》裡出現的薑餅人「Gingerbread man」嗎？就像台灣人中秋節愛吃月餅一樣，在聖誕節享用 gingerbread cookies（薑餅）、gingerbread cake（薑餅蛋糕）也是美國人的習俗。星巴克還會推出期間限定的 gingerbread latte。順帶一提，eggnog（蛋酒）也是聖誕節必喝的飲料之一！

TAIGLISH 「拐杖糖」正確的英文怎麼說？

「拐杖糖」是聖誕節絕對不能漏掉的元素之一。很多人會把拐杖糖直譯成 stick candy，正確的說法其實是 candy cane。拐杖糖大多是薄荷（peppermint）口味，正是最能代表聖誕節的口味之一。

EXPRESSION Right on!

表示強烈贊同，有「好、對」等含義，也可以解釋為「做得好」，表示激勵和支持之意。

Right on, Lora!
這就對了，蘿拉！

You got an A+? Right on!
你得了 A+？做得好！

Every dog has its day
每個人都有走運的時候

表示不管是誰都有走運的時候，也一定會遇到屬於自己的機會，寫成 Every dog has his day. 也無妨。這句話源自於莎士比亞的《哈姆雷特》，時至今日仍是母語使用者愛用的片語之一，似乎證明了即使歷經時代更迭，人們依然懷抱著希望而活。

Tyler How are you holding up? How's your depression?

Jane I'm no longer suicidal, but I'm still on medication.

Tyler Everyone goes through depression at one point in their lives. I don't want you to think you are different.

Jane I was too caught up with success and got impatient. Well, 💬 **every dog has its day.**

Tyler Absolutely! Your time will come but health comes first.

泰勒 妳還好嗎？憂鬱症怎麼樣了？

珍 我已經不再有自殺傾向了，不過仍在接受藥物治療。

泰勒 每個人都多少經歷過憂鬱的症狀，我不希望妳覺得自己是異類。

珍 都是因為我太執著於成功才越來越焦慮。不過機會總有一天會屬於我的。

泰勒 當然！一定會輪到妳的，不過健康還是第一優先。

EXPRESSION How are you holding up?

「你還撐得住嗎？」，知道對方正處於低潮，這句話會比 How are you? 更適合用來表達關心。類似中文「很辛苦吧，還好嗎？」、「看起來很累，沒事吧？」。切記美國文化中，絕對不可以說 You look tired.，會讓聽者覺得很冒犯，怎麼可以評論別人的外貌、心智狀況。若想表達關心，不妨把這句話記起來。

How are you holding up? Are you feeling better?
你還好嗎？有好點了嗎？

EXPRESSION suicidal

「自殺」是 suicide，搭配動詞 commit，「有想自殺的衝動」用形容詞 suicidal。近來自殺的新聞頻傳，希望大家無論面臨什麼困境，都可以鼓起勇氣面對，不要放棄希望，因為活下去這件事，本身就是給自己最好的禮物！

When you are suicidal, please call 1925.
如發現自己有自殺傾向，請一定要撥打 1925 求助。

EXPRESSION on medication

「藥」的名詞是 medication 或 medicine。所以 on medication 就是指現在正在服用醫生開立的藥物，處於「治療中」的狀態。另外有一個相像但意思卻完全不同的片語—— on the pill，pill 是指「藥丸」沒錯，不過在俚語中則是專指避孕藥，表示有在服用避孕藥。

Are you on any medication?
你有在服用什麼藥物嗎？

EXPRESSION caught up (with/in)

指深深沈迷於某種事物，導致無法思考其他事情的狀態。此外也有被辛苦、複雜的事所累的意思。有「被……糾纏」、「被……席捲」、「被……迷惑」和「沈迷於……」等含義。

I got caught up in the moment so I didn't even hear you come in. 我太過沈浸於當下，沒聽見你進來。	**The politician got caught up in several scandals.** 那個政治人物被許多醜聞纏身。

EXPRESSION Your time will come.

如字面上所示，意謂著「屬於你的時刻終會到來」，用來告訴對方只要再撐一下下，就會輪到他發光發熱了。

Work hard, stay disciplined, and be patient. Your time will come.
努力工作、自律、保持耐心，總有一天會輪到你發光發熱。

Blow one's mind
使某人備受震撼

表示使某人感到極強烈的感動。可以用於表示某事或某人使某人嚇了一大跳；使某人備受感動；某人心情興奮。形容詞是 mind-blowing，意思是十分驚人、使人訝異的。偶爾想説 amazing 又覺得老套的時候，就可以試著運用這個説法！

Trevor　How was the Coldplay concert?

Rachel　It was hands down the best. It was sick!

Trevor　I heard listening to Chris Martin singing live literally 💬 **blows your mind**.

Rachel　Yes, I was blown away.

Trevor　You are so lucky that you got the ticket.

Rachel　I can die happy now.

崔佛　「酷玩樂團」的演唱會怎麼樣？

瑞秋　無庸置疑，真的超讚！

崔佛　我聽説主唱克里斯‧馬丁的現場演唱功力真的很驚人。

瑞秋　沒錯，我跪著聽。

崔佛　妳能搶到票真的很幸運。

瑞秋　現在我可以含笑而終了。

IDIOM hands down

用不到手，所以把手放低，表示「不費舉手之勞、非常容易」。也有「無疑地」、「明明白白地」的意思。

It's hands down the best song I've ever heard in my life.
這絕對是我這輩子聽過最好聽的歌。

Trump: We can win this election hands down.
川普：我們可以輕鬆拿下這場選舉。

SLANG sick

演唱會生病？才不是！sick 表示「生病」的意思之外，俚語跟 cool、awesome、crazy 一樣可以拿來表示「太讚了」、「太厲害了」等意思；在英式英語也會用 wicked（邪惡的）表示「太棒了」。

This is a sick car! What do you do for a living?
這部車太屌了！你平常是做什麼工作的？

EXPRESSION literally

母語者口說中經常使用的副詞，不過翻譯成「如字面上所説地」，可能不容易理解。應解釋為「名副其實」、「簡直快要」，類似 really（真的）、almost（幾乎），誇張地強調某件事。反義詞是 figuratively（比喻地、象徵地）。

There were literally like 1,000 people there. I'm not even exaggerating.
不誇張，那裡真的有足足一千個人。

I'm literally freezing to death here. Let's just go inside!
我真的快凍死了，我們趕快進去吧！

IDIOM blown away

指留下深刻印象或備受感動，可解釋為「非常開心」、「神魂顛倒」等意思。此外也有「比分大幅落後而落敗」的意思。

Our team got blown away. We lost 10 to 1.
我們的隊伍以 10 比 1 慘敗。

EXPRESSION I can die happy now.

就如同字面上「現在可以開心地死去了」的意思，表示「死了也沒有遺憾」。實現心願或達成理想，表現喜悅之情的時候，就很適合説這句話。

I proposed and she said yes! I can die happy now!
我求婚了，她説好！我就算死也沒有遺憾了！

Sorry doesn't cut (it)

說對不起就夠了嗎？

字面上的意思是「說對不起也無法剪斷超出的線」，意謂著「說對不起是不夠的」。道歉不誠懇而導致怨恨無法排解的時候；受傷太深無法痊癒的時候；對方犯的錯造成無法挽回的後果，光憑一句抱歉無法解決問題的時候，都可以用這句話來表達。道歉應該要真心誠意，不過最好的辦法還是莫過於從頭到尾都不要做出需要道歉的事！

Michael　I'm sorry for what I said. I don't want any hard feelings.

Julia　You need to know 💬 **sorry doesn't always cut it**.

Michael　I really didn't mean to hurt your feelings.

Julia　Actually, I'm not holding a grudge.

Michael　We good, now?

Julia　Yes! I forgive you!

麥克　我為我說的話向妳道歉，希望妳別生氣。

茱莉亞　你要知道，有些事道歉是沒有用的。

麥克　我真的無意傷害妳。

茱莉亞　老實說，我並不怨恨你。

麥克　那我們現在沒事了嗎？

茱莉亞　嗯！我原諒你！

EXPRESSION hard feelings

因為爭執而不滿對方,產生「討厭」和「憤怒」的負面感。類似的說法還有 resentment(憎恨)。

I have no hard feelings towards you. No worries.
我對你沒有負面情緒,別擔心。

EXPRESSION mean to

mean to 和 intend to 的含義相似,表示「打算做~」、「想做~」。後面可以接各種原形動詞做應用。也可以跟本文一樣以否定句表示「不打算做~」。

I didn't mean to cause trouble.
我無意造成困擾。

I've been meaning to ask you. How do you know her?
我一直都想問你,你是怎麼認識她的?

EXPRESSION hurt (one's) feelings

指傷某人的心或讓某人不開心。可以用來表示「傷感情」、「在心上插刀」、「使不愉快」等意思。

Your jokes sometimes hurt people's feelings.
你的玩笑有時候很傷人。

You hurt my feelings and I want space for a while.
你傷了我的感情,我想跟你保持距離一段時間。

EXPRESSION hold a grudge

指對於他人過去犯的錯持續抱有負面情緒或憤怒。也就是「心懷怨恨」,指心裡還留有疙瘩。《咒怨》這部知名日本恐怖片英文片名正是《The Grudge》。

Holding a grudge is like drinking poison.
心懷怨恨就像一種毒藥。

EXPRESSION We good, now?

省略了句子最前面的 Are。在爭執或吵架過後,用來向對方表示「我們之間沒事了吧?」、「我們和好了嗎?」,主要在道歉後使用。

cry one's eyes out
大哭一場

就如字面上的「哭到眼睛都要掉出來」所形容，這個片語是指長時間失控地哭泣。有「大哭」、「哭到眼睛腫起來」等含義。當傷心到難以承受而淚流滿面的時候，就可以用這個片語來表現。

Mike　Hello? Kate, I'm calling since I heard your grandma passed away.

Kate　Oh, Mike. Thank you. I've been 💬 **crying my eyes out**.

Mike　I'm so sorry for your loss. My condolences.

Kate　In a way I'm glad she is in peace now. She battled cancer for too long.

Mike　You know she is in a better place now.

Kate　Yes, true. I'll be seeing her again, right?

麥可　喂？凱特，我打來是聽說妳奶奶過世了。

凱特　噢，麥克，謝謝你，我眼睛都快哭瞎了。

麥可　很遺憾，請節哀順變。

凱特　從另一方面來說，我也很高興她終於歸於平靜，她跟癌症搏鬥太久了。

麥可　妳應該知道奶奶已經去了更好的地方了吧。

凱特　是，沒錯。我會再見到她的，對吧？

EXPRESSION **pass away**

比起直接的 died（死了），我個人比較喜歡委婉的 pass away 或 gone 等隱喻式表達方式。pass away 是「逝去」，語感上較為溫和慎重。我相信讀者一定能理解這種語感上的差異。

使用 pass 的各種片語動詞

pass 通過；經過；跳過	**pass out** 昏倒；分發	**pass by** 路過
pass through 通過；經歷	**pass on** 傳承；傳達	**pass over** 忽略

EXPRESSION **I am sorry for your loss. / My condolences.**

兩種說法都是為他人的死亡致哀時，一定會用到的說法。有「節哀順變」、「以表悼念」、「為故人的冥福祈禱」等含義。

I offer my deepest condolences to people who are affected by this tragedy.
我向受到這場悲劇影響的人們致上最深的哀悼。

EXPRESSION **Rest in peace (R.I.P.)**

「安詳地入睡」，表示「息止安所」。是墓碑上常見的銘文，傳達祝願逝者安詳長眠的心意。

May Black Panther rest in peace.
願《黑豹》男主角永享安寧。

EXPRESSION **a better place**

A better place 就如字面上的意思，指的是「更好的地方」；但從另一角度看，也代表「死後的世界」，也就是「再也沒有痛苦和悲傷的世界」。

I'm in a better place than last year.
我今年比去年進步了。

If you care enough for the living, make a better place for you and me.
如果你也關懷生命，我們就一起為彼此創造更美好的世界吧。　　──麥可傑克森《Heal the world》

EXPRESSION **I'll be seeing you.**

I'll be seeing you. 和 I'll see you. 的語氣不同。這個片語與 Goodbye. 相似，大多表示接下來會長期見不到面，或還不確定下次見面是什麼時候。

Let's Practice!
DAY 61-70

Exercise 1 請用題目中給的單字造句。

1. 你還好嗎？過得怎樣？（hold）
_____

2. 演唱會真的太驚豔了，讓我神魂顛倒。（my mind）
_____

3. 我喜歡與人相處。（people）
_____

4. 我大哭一場。（eyes）
_____

5. 我無意傷你的感情。（your feelings）
_____

6. 節哀順變。（My）
_____

7. 這無疑是最好的。（hands）
_____

8. 我在放空。（zone）
_____

9. 我不喜歡欲擒故縱。（hard to）
_____

10. 我常聽人那麼跟我說。（get）
_____

解答 1
1) How are you holding up?　2) The concert blew my mind.　3) I'm a people person.　4) I cried my eyes out.　5) I didn't mean to hurt your feelings.　6) My condolences.　7) It was hands down the best.　8) I zoned out.　9) I don't like playing hard to get.　10) I get that a lot.

1. 酒量不好的人

Cheap _____

2. 太讚了！

It was _____!

3. 我沒天分。

I'm not cut _____.

4. 說對不起是不夠的。

Sorry _____.

5. 你看起來很年輕。

You look _____.

6. 即將來臨！

Just _____!

7. 酸民留言

_____ comments

8. 人總會有走運的一天。

_____ its day.

9. 姻緣天注定，有一天會找到對象。

Every Jack _____.

10. 我洗耳恭聽。

I'm all _____.

解答 2
1) drunk   2) sick   3) out for it   4) doesn't cut (it)   5) young for your age   6) around the corner
7) Hateful   8) Every dog has   9) has his Jill   10) ears

Make ends meet
勉強維生

指雖然沒有負債，但收入勉強可以糊口的狀態。意思是收支平衡，賺的錢剛好可以應付生活費。

Frank   I'm barely 💬 **making ends meet** these days due to COVID.

Lora   Same here. I'm literally living hand to mouth.

Frank   I also heard Kyle's company went out of business.

Lora   I'm not surprised because he had been making peanuts for years.

Frank   Well, all of us will get through this, though.

Lora   Let's stay strong! Life isn't always peaches and cream.

法蘭克   我最近因為 COVID-19 收支很緊繃。

蘿拉   我也是，賺的錢勉強能糊口。

法蘭克   我聽說凱爾的公司也倒閉了。

蘿拉   我不意外，因為他已經好幾年沒賺到錢了。

法蘭克   嗯，不過我們總會度過難關的。

蘿拉   撐下去吧！畢竟人生本來就不是童話故事。

EXPRESSION **Same here.**

想要表達「我也是。」，除了 Me too. 之外還有其他選擇，例如 Same. / Same here. / So do I. / Likewise. / Me as well. 等。趁這個機會擺脱 Me too. 這個老套的説法吧！

IDIOM **living hand to mouth**

「賺到的錢馬上就進了嘴巴」，指一天的收入剛好應付一日所需。比 making ends meet 的經濟狀況更困難，「光是糊口都很不容易」的意思。

Many of self-made millionaires have the experience of living hand to mouth.
許多白手起家的百萬富翁都曾經歷過收入僅能勉強度日的階段。

IDIOM **make peanuts**

peanuts 表示「微薄的小錢」，所以這個片語就是指「收入微薄」；除了 make 之外，動詞也可以搭配 earn 和 pay。而 work for peanuts 則是表示「工作收入低得不像話」。

I'm sick and tired of working for peanuts. I'm done! 辛苦工作卻只賺得這麼一點錢，我受夠了！	**If you pay peanuts you get monkeys.** 你只付香蕉，那就只請得到猴子。

EXPRESSION **stay strong**

stay strong 是「保持堅強」，意謂著「即使身處困境也不被打倒或擊潰，持續堅守下去」，表示「堅強地撐下去」。

Stay strong for me. Don't ever give up. 為了我努力撐下去吧，別放棄。	**His family stayed strong as one and eventually got through it.** 他的家人很團結，一起熬過了困境。

IDIOM **peaches and cream**

指白裡透紅的「滑嫩肌膚」，也可以用來表示「沒有任何問題，一切順暢愉快」。

She has got peaches and cream complexion. 她的皮膚白裡透紅。	**He acts like everything is peaches and cream but actually it's not.** 他一副所有問題迎刃而解的樣子，其實並不然。

This is my cup of tea
這是我的菜

跟「這是我的菜」、「這很合我胃口」一樣，這個片語是用來形容自己喜歡事物的傾向。我們遇到喜歡的類型有時會説「他是我的 style」，而英文裡的 my style 雖然可以用來表示自己的喜好，但其實不會用來形容對人的偏好，反而要解釋為「我本來就是這種風格」的意思才對。如果遇到自己喜歡的類型，就用 my type 或 my cup of tea 來表示吧！

Alison   This place has cheesecake to die for.

Lora   I love cheesecake! 💬 **This is so my cup of tea!**

Alison   I didn't know you have a sweet tooth too.

Lora   Are you kidding? I can't live without desserts.

Alison   You are my partner in crime now.

Lora   Fabulous, we will try every good dessert place in town!

艾莉森   這裡的起司蛋糕真是絕了。

蘿拉   我很愛起司蛋糕！這完全是我的菜！

艾莉森   沒想到妳也是螞蟻人。

蘿拉   開什麼玩笑？我不吃甜點活不下去。

艾莉森   那現在起我們就是姐妹了。

蘿拉   太棒了，我們一起征服這附近所有的甜點店吧！

EXPRESSION **to die for**

表示喜歡某件事物到「值得為其獻上生命」、「值得拿命去換」。是不正式的說法，常出現在口語中用來加強語氣，可以解釋為「非常迷人」、「了不起」、「漂亮」等意思。

Wow! That's a diamond to die for!
哇！那顆鑽石太美了！

How do you make these to-die-for barbeques?
你是怎麼做出這麼好吃的烤肉的？

IDIOM **have a sweet tooth**

指「嗜吃甜食」。tooth 是「一顆牙齒」，所以前面一定要加冠詞 a。

Do you have a sweet tooth?
你愛吃甜食嗎？

I don't really have a sweet tooth. I'm not a dessert person.
我不喜歡甜的東西，對甜點不感興趣。

PATTERN **can't live without + 名詞**

「沒有～就活不下去」，表示非常喜歡、熱愛某事物。也可以如字面上的意思所示，缺乏某種東西就無法存活，例如：「我們沒有空氣就活不下去」。

I can't live without you.
沒有你我活不下去。

Humans can't live without water, air and food.
人類沒有水、空氣、食物會活不下去。

EXPRESSION **partner in crime**

原意指「共犯」，也有「最好的朋友」的含義。最要好的老朋友正是一起犯錯、一起像傻瓜一樣闖禍的最佳拍檔啊。

We used to always get in trouble in high school together.

He is my partner in crime.
我們高中時老是一起惹麻煩，他是我的好麻吉。

Jeff and his manager were partners in crime. They both got fired.
傑夫和他的經理是共犯，他們兩個都被炒魷魚了。

You are what you eat
人如其食

這句話是指人吃了什麼、吃了多少食物，都會直接反映在身體健康上。「你就是你吃的食物」，表示健康的飲食能使身體健康，不良好的飲食習慣則對健康有害。別忘了，攝取對身體有益的食物也是寵愛自己的方式之一！

Kate	I have constant migraines these days.
Tom	That's too bad! Do you get regular health checkups?
Kate	Yeah, I do. I just haven't been eating properly.
Tom	You really have a poor eating habit. 💬 **You are what you eat.**
Kate	I know.
Tom	You are technically made of what you eat. So if you eat bad you feel bad and look bad.

凱特	我最近老是偏頭痛。
湯姆	怎麼會！妳有定期做健康檢查嗎？
凱特	我有。我只是最近吃得不太正常。
湯姆	妳的飲食習慣真的很差。妳吃的東西都會反映在妳身上。
凱特	我知道。
湯姆	嚴格來說，妳的身體就是由妳吃的食物所組成的。如果妳不好好吃飯，妳不只會不舒服，還會變得不好看。

migraine vs. headache

migraine（偏頭痛）是 headache（頭痛）的類型之一。偏頭痛大部分是指包含眼部的頭部某側感到疼痛，也可能伴隨暈眩、對聲音或光線敏感的症狀。migraine 跟 headache 一樣屬於可數名詞。

EXPRESSION **That's too bad!**

對於某個問題感同身受時，用來表示「太糟了」、「怎麼會」、「好可惜」等含義的片語。類似的說法還有 I'm sorry.（我很遺憾）。但要注意，依據語氣和表情的不同，也可以諷刺表達「活該」的意思。

It's too bad that you can't make it today. 真可惜妳今天不能來。

A: I cracked my phone screen. 我把手機螢幕摔裂了。

B: Oh no! That's too bad! 天啊！怎麼會！

MOST ASKED **「定期健康檢查」正確的英文怎麼說？**

很多人都想知道定期健檢該怎麼說！正是 regular health checkup。checkup 有「檢查」、「身體檢查」或是「檢驗」的意思。

I go to my doctor for regular checkups.
我去找我的醫師做定期健檢。

Simple car checkups on a daily basis save lives.
每天簡單檢查一下車輛可以保障生命安全。

EXPRESSION **technically**

字面上是「技術地」，不過在口語中更常用來表示「嚴格來說」、「正確地說」，是母語使用者經常掛在嘴邊的轉折語（transition）之一。

Korea is technically very advanced.
韓國在技術方面十分發達。

Technically, it's my laptop because I paid for it but my brother uses it most of the time.
嚴格來說，那是我的電腦，因為是我花錢買的，不過大部分的時間都是我弟弟在用。

Day 73

Tie the knot
結婚

可以按照字面上的意思表示「打結」，不過 knot（繩結）象徵 unity（結為一體），以此比喻兩人結為連理，引申為「結婚」、「締結婚約」的意思。類似的說法還有 marry，不過要注意表示「和某人結婚」時，marry 後面不加介系詞 with。I married Bob.（我跟鮑伯結婚了）才是正確的說法。

Taylor	Sam and Sarah are finally 💬 **tying the knot**!
Lora	Wow, really? They both have hearts of gold. I love them both.
Taylor	We should plan a bridal shower and a bachelorette party for Sarah.
Lora	Are you the maid of honor?
Taylor	Yes, and you are the bridesmaid.
Lora	Let's go all out to make this wedding special!

泰勒	山姆和莎拉終於結婚了！
蘿拉	哇，真的嗎？他們心地都很好，我很喜歡他們。
泰勒	我們應該要幫莎拉準備婚前聚會跟單身派對。
蘿拉	妳是主伴娘嗎？
泰勒	對，妳是伴娘。
蘿拉	我們要使出渾身解數，創造一場終身難忘的婚禮！

IDIOM **a heart of gold**

「如黃金般高貴的心」，表示心地善良，為他人著想，對有困難的人伸出援手的善良之人。用法類似我們以美玉譬喻人的品性純淨高潔。

He has a heart of gold. He is a very giving person.
他心地很善良，願意為他人付出。

CULTURE **bridal shower**

女性好友為即將結婚的新娘舉辦的聚會，贈送禮物給新娘致上賀意。bridal shower 只限女性參加，而 wedding shower 雖然與其用意相同，但不限性別，所有人都能參加。

CULUTURE **bachelorette party**

指「女生在結婚前夕一起開的派對」。我們一般比較常聽到 bachelor party（單身漢派對）。結婚前最後一次以單身的身分，狂歡一整夜，規模可大可小，小至一般夜店，大至拉斯維加斯，都是常見的單身派對地點。

For my bachelorette party I just want to have a spa night with my girls.
我只想跟好姐妹們一起做 spa 度過我的單身女郎派對。

CULTURE **maid of honor**

「新娘的伴娘」是 bridesmaid，而最親的朋友則可以列為 maid of honor，作為主伴娘幫助新娘在籌備婚禮的過程中做決策。男方伴郎稱為 groomsman，而新郎最要好的朋友則是 best-man，同樣也會扮演新郎的左右手，幫忙打理婚禮中的大小事。

One of the duties for the maid of honor is to plan a bridal shower.
主伴娘的任務之一就是策劃婚前聚會。

IDIOM **go all out**

「全力以赴」，指「傾其所有」。all in 有在玩撲克牌時賭上所有籌碼的意思，也可以用來表示身體疲倦。所以要表達本文中「賭上我的一切，全力以赴做到最好」之意時，還是用 go all out 最為合適。

If you really want it, you have to go all out.
如果你真的想要的話，那你必須傾盡全力去獲得。

I'm going to have an extremely extravagant wedding. I'm really gonna go all out.
我要辦一場極盡奢華的婚宴，不惜砸上一切。

Jump out of one's skin
大吃一驚

靈魂就像蛇脫皮一樣被嚇到從身體裡跑出來，意指聽到巨響或好消息而被嚇得跳起來，或因為恐懼而嚇得直發抖。

Jeff	Let's go to the movies tonight.
Lora	Don't tell me you want to watch a horror movie again. I literally  **jumped out of my skin** last time.
Jeff	But I've been waiting for this movie for so long.
Lora	Don't even try to talk me into watching it this time.
Jeff	I watch those boring tear jerkers with you every time. Those make me cringe!

傑夫	今天晚上我們去看電影吧。
蘿拉	不要跟我說你又要看恐怖電影哦。上次我真的嚇慘了。
傑夫	但是我等這部電影等很久耶。
蘿拉	你這次別想說服我。
傑夫	我每次都陪妳看那些無聊灑狗血的芭樂片，看得超無言的！

SPOKEN ENGLISH **go to the movies**

字面上是「去電影」，也就是「去看電影」的意思。雖然 go to the movie theater 是正確的說法，但是 go to the movies 更自然，go see a movie 也經常使用。

I went to the movies last night.
昨晚我去看電影。

I want to go see a movie.
我想去看電影。

PATTERN **Don't tell me ＋ 名詞子句**

「別告訴我～」，此句型用在不相信對方說的話，有「你該不會～吧？」、「你是騙人的吧？」等意思。

Don't tell me you lost the key.
你該不會弄丟你的鑰匙吧？

PATTERN **talk (someone) into ＋ 動名詞**

意為說服對方，使其作出某種行為。相反地，說服對方不要或放棄做某事則是「talk (someone) out of ＋動名詞」。

I think I can talk her into it. Just give me some time.
我想我能夠說服她，只是要給我一點時間。

EXPRESSION **tear jerker**

「催淚彈」意指灑狗血，刻意讓人悲傷流淚的小說、歌曲或電影。

I'm not much of a fan of tear jerker movies. I prefer action.
我不愛那種悲情灑狗血的芭樂電影，我比較喜歡動作片。

MOST ASKED **「覺得尷尬到難為情」正確的英文怎麼說？**

「尷尬」、「難為情」的英語就是 makes me cringe。cringe 有「嚇得蜷縮」，感到恐懼、嫌惡、羞恥、尷尬、無言等意思。

My past behavior makes me cringe.
我過去的行為讓我感到羞恥。

It makes me cringe to listen to my own voice.
我聽自己的聲音感覺好不舒服。

I have bigger fish to fry
有更重要的事

我要炸一條更大的魚？這裡的 fish 是指「事情」或「約定」的意思。可以用在有更有意義的事要做，或是有更重要的約會，又或是不想浪費時間和精力在不重要的事情時，就可以使用。fish 不寫成複數 fishes，這很容易搞混，一定要記得！bigger 也可以替換成 better 或 other。

Mylo   Is Lisa still mad at you?

Bell   Apparently. We haven't spoken for 6 months now.

Mylo   Oh geez. Lisa is such a drama queen.

Bell   Uh huh, she surely likes to stir the pot.

Mylo   You know what, you might be better off without her.

Bell   It's really not worth my time. 💬 **I have bigger fish to fry**.

米洛   麗莎還在生妳的氣嗎？

貝爾   很明顯啊。我們已經六個月沒講話了。

米洛   天啊，麗莎真的很浮誇耶。

貝爾   對啊，她很愛把事情弄得很複雜。

米洛   妳知道嗎？沒有她，妳會更好。

貝爾   我還有大事要做，沒空理她。

EXPRESSION **apparently**

「如你所見」、「顯然地」的意思，可以用在無法百分之百確定自己說的資訊，或並未熟知具體的內容時。要記得的是，形容詞 apparent 是「明顯」的意思，和副詞 apparently 的語感很不一樣。

Apparently he was in a hurry.
顯然他很急。

EXCLAMATION **Geez!**

感嘆詞，也可寫成 jeez，用來表達驚訝、煩躁、無奈等情緒，相當於「天啊」、「哎呀」、「吼唷」等。類似的說法還有 God! 和 Gosh!。

Jeez, don't yell at me!
天啊，不要對我大吼大叫！

Geez! You scared the hell out of me!
媽呀！你嚇死我了！

EXPRESSION **drama queen**

看舞台劇的時候，可以看到比較誇張的演技，這個詞就是拿來形容反應很浮誇的「女人」。指為了刷存在感，像悲情的女主角般哭哭啼啼，或是滿腹牢騷，只要有點累就哭得好像世界末日，一點小事就搞得像在拍一齣電視劇一樣的人。如果身邊有這種人，就會覺得對方很難搞、想敬而遠之，算是帶有負面意思的詞。

I can't keep calm because I'm a drama queen.
我無法冷靜，因為我就是很戲劇化的人。

IDIOM **stir the pot**

指製造不必要的爭執，也有故意煽風點火、挑撥離間等意思。

Please don't stir the pot. Don't bring up the past.
拜託別刻意製造紛爭，不要翻舊帳。

EXPRESSION **better off**

意指在心理上、經濟上「處於較好的狀況」，〈better off ＋動名詞〉也經常拿來表達「……做更好」的句型。

You crack me up
你真的太好笑了

crack 雖然是「龜裂」、「裂開」的意思，但是當作名詞時，也有「毒品」的意思。因此這個成語可以想成好笑到像用了毒品般瘋癲、神智不清，會更好理解。當對方太好笑，讓你笑出來或捧腹大笑時，就可以使用這個片語哦。

Bella	Stop dancing in class! Are you on crack?
Jeff	You don't know BTS? They are a thing now.
Bella	💬 **You crack me up** so bad. You should be a comedian.
Jeff	I'm gonna audition for a boy band.
Bella	Dream on!

貝拉	上課時間別跳舞了！你瘋了哦！
傑夫	妳不知道 BTS 嗎？他們很夯耶。
貝拉	你真的要讓我笑死了，你應該去當諧星。
傑夫	我要去甄選男子偶像團體。
貝拉	醒醒吧你！

SLANG Are you on crack?

如前所述，crack 是指「毒品」的意思，因此「你嗑藥嗎？」就可以用在對方的舉動或對方說的話讓你感到無言、衝擊，且難以置信時，和 Are you crazy?（你瘋了嗎？）是一樣的意思。

I can't believe you stole that. You are on crack!
我不敢相信你竟然偷了那個，你瘋了！

IDIOM a thing

某人與某人之間有什麼，即「有一腿」、「有曖昧」的意思，也指大幅傳播的「流行」，受歡迎的意思。也會用在強調 anything，是「任何事」的意思。

I don't want to miss a thing.
〈我不願錯過這一切〉

——Aerosmith 史密斯飛船歌曲名稱

UGG boots are a thing now.
UGG 雪靴最近很紅。

Apparently they have a thing.
顯然他們在搞曖昧。

EXPRESSION so bad

這不是「很壞」的意思，而是像「very」或「really」一樣強調前面提到的東西。

I want pizza so bad.
我超想吃披薩。

I wanna go home so bad.
我超想回家。

CULTURE 美國喜劇種類

comedian（喜劇演員）源自 comedy（喜劇），依類別分為：situation comedy (sitcom) 情境喜劇；romantic comedy (romcom) 浪漫喜劇；tragic comedy (tragicomedy) 悲喜劇。近來流行的「單口喜劇」稱為 stand-up comedy。

EXPRESSION Dream on!

意為「繼續做夢吧」，也就是絕對無法成真的意思，相當於我們說的「少做夢」、「醒醒吧」。

You really thought I like you? Dream on!
你真的以為我喜歡你？醒醒吧！

At the end of the day
最後、最終

雖然字面上是「一天的尾聲」的意思,但是在日常生活中,抑或商業場合,都很常拿來當作「最後」、「最終」、「結論是」的意思,也就是「最後最重要的事」。網路常縮寫成「@TEOTD」。

Lora	It is so heartbreaking to see so much hate and segregation in our society today.
Kay	True, racism is getting out of hand these days.
Lora	💬 **At the end of the day** there is just one race I believe, which is the human race.
Kay	Because we are human beings we tend to have bigotry by nature.
Lora	That is why we need to constantly teach and learn that racism is ignorant.
Kay	I strongly agree that education can change the world. We all need anti-racism education!

蘿拉	看到現今社會有那麼多憎恨和歧視,就覺得心痛。
凱	沒錯,最近種族歧視的情況真的很失控。
蘿拉	我相信最終只會有一個種族存在,就是人類。
凱	因為我們是人類,所以天生就有偏見。
蘿拉	這也是為什麼我們必須持續教育和學習種族歧視是一種無知。
凱	我非常同意教育可以改變世界,我們都需要反種族歧視的教育。

segregation

意指「隔離」、「區分」、「分離」，但通常指的是宗教、人種、性別等「歧視」，刻意隔離族群。而 separation 指「（夫妻）分居」、「（領土）分裂」。

Segregation of Whites and colored people was outlawed in 1954.
1954 年白人和有色人種的隔離政策被宣判為非法。

get out of hand

意為太誇張或太嚴重而導致「束手無策」的意思，類似的說法還有 out of control，相反詞為 under control。

Kids were getting out of hand at the playground.
孩子們在遊樂場大失控。

Is everything under control?
一切還順利嗎？

He gets out of control when he is drunk.
他如果喝醉就會失控。

PATTERN tend to ＋原形動詞

表達「有～的傾向」、「往往容易～」的句型，後面接原形動詞。

I tend to get grouchy when I'm hungry.
當我餓了，我人就會變得很機車。

Jenny tends to pig out when she gets under a lot of stress.
珍妮如果壓力太大，容易暴飲暴食。

EXPRESSION bigotry

意指「嚴重的偏見」，比 prejudice 的語感強烈。bigotry 比較接近不當的個人想法和信仰，厭惡某些特定的人或團體，大部分指對其他宗教和種族有偏見和仇恨。

Bigotry is a serious disease in our society.
偏見在我們的社會中是很嚴重的病。

We all need to try to overcome any forms of bigotry.
我們必須努力克服任何形式的偏見。

Total package
人生勝利組

如字面上所說，就是「整包好好」，具備一切所需的特質，外表突出，個性
又好，連家庭背景也很完美的「人生勝利組」，就像媽媽很愛跟我們說隔壁
阿姨家的兒子或女兒有多棒棒一樣。

Jay	I think I'm starting to have feelings for Sarah. She is really fun to be with.
Anna	Sarah? She is a 💬 **total package**!
Jay	I know. She is totally out of my league.
Anna	You are the real deal. I don't know what you are talking about.
Jay	I feel like she's too good for me.
Anna	Oh, come on! Don't be a chicken!

傑	我覺得我好像有點喜歡莎拉，跟她在一起真的很開心。
安娜	莎拉？她超完美！
傑	我知道，我根本配不上她。
安娜	你很棒！你在瞎說什麼！
傑	我覺得她對我來說太好了。
安娜	拜託！別那麼孬！

EXPRESSION have feelings for

指「有感覺」的意思，但不是火熱地愛著某個人。這裡的 feelings 不是單純「感覺」的意思，也包含「喜歡的情感」在內。當自己對已經分手的戀人還有所留戀時，也常使用這個片語。

I still have feelings for Henry.
我對亨利還是有感覺。

IDIOM out of my league

字面上的意思是「在我聯盟之外」，也就是「超過我能承擔的範圍」的意思。可以用在某人事物，遠遠超過自己的水準所及，不適合自己的時候。

Harvard law school was way out of my league.
哈佛法學院實在非我能力所及。

EXPRESSION real deal

字面意思是「真的交易」，指有價值的交易，依照情境可形容「很優秀厲害的人」、「真誠老實的人」或「有價值的物品」，也有「事實真相」等意思。

My relationship with Ken is the real deal.
我和肯的關係是認真的。

So what's the real deal?
所以真相是什麼？

EXPRESSION too good for someone

超過自己的資格，即「配不上」。for 如果改成 to，意思會改變，too good to me 是「對我太好了」的意思，千萬不要搞混囉！

If you think he's too good for you then try to be good enough for him.
如果你覺得配不上他，那就努力成為配得上他的人吧。

SLANG chicken

chicken 是「雞」，也有「膽小鬼」的意思。chicken out 則有因為被嚇到而放棄的意思。

I'm such a chicken when it comes to driving.
每當開車我就變膽小鬼了。

I chickened out due to fear of rejection.
我害怕被拒絕，所以就放棄了。

Whatever floats your boat
愛怎麼做就怎麼做

意為「朝著你覺得幸福，內心想走的方向去做」、「愛怎麼做就怎麼做」、「隨心所欲」、「只要你好我就好」。當不在意吃什麼、做什麼的時候就可以使用，不但不會沒禮貌，反而還帶點幽默感。類似的成語還有 Whatever makes you happy、Whatever tickles your pickle 等。

Bob Where do you want to go for our dinner tonight? I'm in charge.

Lora I'm the most indecisive person.

Bob Cheesecake factory?

Lora You are asking the wrong person. 💬 **Whatever floats your boat.**

Bob You are no help.

Lora Anything works the best for everyone.

鮑伯 今天晚餐妳想去哪裡吃？我負責處理。

蘿拉 我是最沒主見的人了。

鮑伯 起司蛋糕工廠？

蘿拉 你問錯人了，你決定哪裡就哪裡吧。

鮑伯 妳真的沒什麼幫助。

蘿拉 只要大家好就好囉。

MOST ASKED 「聚餐」的正確英語怎麼說？

美國幾乎沒有下班聚餐的文化，通常都是邀請好友到家裡辦派對。如果硬要講的話，可直接使用 dinner。staff party 則接近例如聖誕節、過年等特別的日子，公司辦的聚餐。其他為了拉近同事關係的活動，用 team building 或 team get-together 更適合。記住，語言和文化密不可分哦！

I have dinner with my teammates tonight.
我今晚要和部門同事吃晚餐。

We have Christmas staff party this Friday.
這星期五我們公司有聖誕派對。

EXPRESSION in charge

和 responsible 一樣，指負責某事的意思。

Who's in charge of this?
是誰負責這個？

I'm in charge of HR.
我是人資的負責人。

MOST ASKED 「優柔寡斷」的英文是？

decide 是動詞，為「決定」、「選擇」的意思，形容詞 decisive 則意為「可以做決定，明確知道自己想要什麼」；相反地，優柔寡斷的人，即「無法下決定的人」，則可以説 indecisive。

You still haven't decided what to wear? Stop being so indecisive!
你還沒決定要穿什麼嗎？
不要再猶豫不決了！

You can't be indecisive about this anymore. Make up your mind!
這件事你不能再優柔寡斷了！快下定決心！

EXPRESSION You are asking the wrong person.

你問不對人？也就是「你問到不適合回答問題的人」，背後的意思是「我也不知道」。相反地，問對人就是 You are asking the right person.。

A: **Do you know how to apply for schools in America?**
你知道怎麼申請美國的學校嗎？

B: **You are asking the right person! I went to college in the states.**
你問對人了！我在美國念過大學。

Let's Practice!
DAY 71-80

Exercise 1　請用題目中給的單字造句。

1. 這是我的菜。（tea）

_____

2. 我嚇到魂飛魄散了。（I jumped）

_____

3. 別那麼孬！（chicken）

_____

4. 你真的很搞笑。（crack）

_____

5. 你想怎樣就怎樣囉。（float）

_____

6. 她心地很善良。（gold）

_____

7. 種族歧視越來越嚴重。（out of）

_____

8. 我有更重要的事要做。（fish）

_____

9. 這讓我感到難為情。（It makes）

_____

10. 人生本來就不是童話故事。（peaches）

_____

解答 1

1) This is my cup of tea.　2) I jumped out of my skin.　3) Don't be a chicken!　4) You crack me up.
5) Whatever floats your boat.　6) She has heart of gold.　7) Racism is getting out of hand.
8) I have bigger fish to fry.　9) It makes me cringe.　10) Life isn't always peaches and cream.

Exercise 2 依照句意填入正確答案。

1. 他是人生勝利組。

He is a _____.

2. 收支平衡

Make _____

3. 你吃什麼，就像什麼。

_____ eat.

4. 超有事的悲情女主角

Drama _____

5. 最終、最重要的事

At the _____

6. 結婚

Tied _____

7. 灑狗血的芭樂劇

_____ jerker

8. 那真是太慘了！

_____ too _____!

9. 讚到讓人願意付出性命

To _____

10. 要保持堅強！

Stay _____!

解答 2

1) total package   2) ends meet   3) You are what you   4) queen

5) end of the day   6) the knot   7) Tear   8) That's, bad   9) die for   10) strong

Brush it off!
別理會！

大家有看過美國人像拍掉灰塵一樣拍肩的手勢嗎？那個姿勢就叫做 brush one's shoulders off，和 brush it off 是一樣的意思。意為如果有人說我壞話或讓我感到不悅時，不需要太在意，就像撣掉灰塵一樣，拋諸腦後或直接忽視即可。希望大家此刻都能把所有負面想法和負能量全都 brush it off!（全都拋開吧！）

Esther	I had the rudest customer come in today.
Robin	Yuck, one of those days, huh? I'm sorry.
Esther	I'm trying to  **brush it off**.
Robin	Do whatever it takes to chillax tonight. It's just a bad day, not a bad life.
Esther	True. Shit happens!
Robin	Yes, always! Let's laugh it off!

伊瑟	今天來了個超級奧客。
羅賓	呃，真倒霉，對吧？我為妳感到難過。
伊瑟	我正在努力忘掉。
羅賓	無論如何，今晚就好好冷靜和放鬆，妳只是今天觸衰，不代表一輩子都會觸衰。
伊瑟	沒錯，難免會踩到屎！
羅賓	是不是！笑笑就算了！

EXCLAMATION Yuck!

表達噁心或嫌惡的感嘆詞，類似的用法還有 Eww!。

Yuck! This smells like rotten eggs!
噁！這聞起來就像壞掉的蛋！

IDIOM one of those days

人生在世難免會發生不如意的事，以及犯下奇怪的失誤。這個片語「那些日子之一」的意思，也就是前面提到的「不如意又倒霉的日子」。

A: How was your day today?
你今天過得如何？

B: I had one of those days. My car wouldn't start in the morning and I cracked my phone screen.
今天很衰。早上我的車發不動，然後我還摔壞手機螢幕。

SLANG chillax

這個字是 chill（休息、冷靜）和 relax（放鬆）的合成語。雖然也是「放鬆心情休息」的意思，但是也跟 chill out 是一樣的意思，意為「冷靜」。

You two need to chillax. Otherwise, I'm calling the cops.
你們倆都給我冷靜，不然我要叫警察了。

I'm gonna sleep in and just chillax at home today.
我今天要睡到飽，然後在家耍廢。

SLANG Shit happens!

意為人生就是會發生各種爛事，而且有「沒辦法，只能接受」的語感。比較好聽的說法就是 Life happens。

EXPRESSION laugh it off

一笑置之的意思，輕鬆看待讓人無言、不愉快的事，和 brush it off 很雷同。

I couldn't laugh his rude jokes off. He was definitely crossing the line.
我無法對他沒禮貌的玩笑一笑置之，他真的太超過了。

When pigs fly
太陽打西邊出來

當豬會飛的時候？你有看過豬在天上飛嗎？當然不可能。這句話的意思就是在比喻發生機率幾近為零，或絕對不可能的意思，相當於「太陽打西邊出來」、「我就把名字倒過來寫」、「天方夜譚」等意思，也可以說 Pigs might fly. 或 When pig have wings.。

Dona　I've been hitting the gym lately and I feel great.

Lora　Have you been lifting weights? You look very toned.

Dona　Yes! I started to get rid of my muffin top. You could tag along.

Lora　I would 💬 **when pigs fly**. Haha. Just kidding.

Dona　Working out has enhanced my mood and improved my self-esteem.

Lora　I want to get rid of these flabby arms too!

多娜　最近我在上健身房，感覺很好。
蘿拉　妳也有練舉重嗎？妳看起來好結實。
多娜　嗯！我是為了減我的腰間肉才開始的，妳可以跟著我做。
蘿拉　我無法……哈哈，開玩笑的啦。
多娜　運動讓我的心情變好，也提升我的自信呢。
蘿拉　我也想減掉我的蝴蝶袖！

EXPRESSION hit the gym

hit 除了「打」，還有「抨擊」、「抵達」、「命中」等各種意思。而 hit the gym 是「上健身房」的意思，等於 go to the gym，但是更口語，生活中也很常使用。

MOST ASKED 健身的說法

一般在健身房運動，英文可以用 work out。weight lifting（舉重）、weight training（重訓）聽起來是比較專業的運動。練身材可說 bodybuilding，練得好的健美運動者稱為 bodybuilder。

EXPRESSION toned

動詞 tone 指「將肌肉鍛鍊得結實有彈性」的意思，因此 toned 是「身材結實」的意思，和 tone 意思相近的片語動詞有 firm up。

Jimmy's got a perfectly toned body. I'm so jealous!
吉米有完美結實的身材，好羨慕哦！

SLANG muffin top

用來指從褲頭擠出來的腰間贅肉，看起來就像瑪芬的上半部，也就是我們説的「游泳圈」，類似的俚語還有 love handles（愛的手把）。

I do sit ups every day to get rid of love handles.
為了減掉游泳圈，我每天都做仰臥起坐。

EXPRESSION tag along

tag 是「標籤」的意思，就像中文會説「貼標籤」一樣，這個片語就是「黏在後面」的意思，尤其用來説不請自來，跟著某個人的行為。

Can I tag along?
我可以跟嗎？

My little sister wants to tag along everywhere I go.
我妹是跟屁蟲，走到哪跟到哪。

EXPRESSION flabby

flabby 意為「無力的」、「沒力氣的」或「下垂的（贅肉）」，所以 flabby 經常拿來描述軟趴趴、毫無彈性可言的蝴蝶袖或腹部贅肉。

I want to firm up my flabby tummy.
我想讓肚子的肥肉變結實。

It's (all) Greek to me
聽得霧煞煞

如果在英語圈國家說希臘語會怎麼樣？當然是沒人聽得懂啊。字面上是「對我來說是希臘語」，相當於「我不懂」、「一竅不通」、「就等於在跟我說外國話一樣」、「天書」等意思。這個用法最早出現在莎士比亞的劇作《凱薩大帝》（The Tragedy of Julius Caesar）。

Lora	Everyone is talking about the US presidential election but 💬 **it's all Greek to me.**
Tim	Which part don't you understand?
Lora	I heard Hilary couldn't win even though she won the popular vote last election.
Tim	Oh, you are talking about the electoral college.
Lora	Yeah, it is so confusing!
Tim	Because of this system it is crucial to win the key swing states.

蘿拉	大家都在談美國總統大選，但是我根本不懂。
提姆	哪一部分不懂？
蘿拉	我聽說希拉蕊不會當選，即使她贏了上次的普選。
提姆	啊～妳是在說選舉人團啊。
蘿拉	嗯，好讓人困惑！
提姆	因為這項制度，拿下搖擺州是關鍵。

美國總統選舉

美國並不是由 electorate（一般選民）直接選出自己想要的總統，而是由 electoral college（選舉人團）先投票選出總統，而選舉人團是按該州人口的比例選出來的。像加州人口數最多，有 55 位選舉人，而選舉人一共有 538 人。因此，即使 popular vote（普選）或 poll（民調）顯示的支持率高，也可能會輸。

例如，在加州，即使 A 候選人僅贏了一票，55 位 electoral college vote（選舉人團票）也會「全部」給 A，這叫做 winner-take-all（贏者全拿），也就說即使在加州只輸了一票，就等於輸了 55 張選舉人票。而先拿到 270 位選舉人票的 candidate（候選人），就會當選美國總統。美國是聯邦國家，把各州都當成一個個體，就會比較好懂。

EXPRESSION **swing states**

「搖擺州」沒有明顯的政治色彩傾向，因此美國總統選舉，關鍵就在拿下搖擺州，相同的說法還有 battleground states。

This year the key Swing States were Wisconsin, Pennsylvania, Michigan and North Carolina.
今年關鍵的搖擺州有威斯康辛、賓州、密西根，以及北卡羅萊納州。

EXPRESSION **swing voter / floating voter**

swing 是「左右搖擺」，voter 則是「投票者」，所以這個用詞用來指不知道選誰，心裡一直搖擺的選民。相同的說法還有 floating voter。

I do not advocate neither Republican nor Democrat. I'm a swing voter.
我不支持共和黨，也不支持民主黨，我是中間選民。

EXPRESSION **running mate**

指和總統候選人一起參選的「共同參選人」，也就是 vice president（副總統）。

Joe Biden's running mate was Kamala Harris. She became the very first female vice president in the US.
拜登的共同參選人是賀錦麗，她是美國第一位女性副總統。

Have hiccups
有小麻煩

雖然 hiccup 是「打嗝」的意思，口語上可以用來比喻「不大也不嚴重的小問題或困難」，也就是大部分可以輕易解決的事。來看看在飯店或住處發生問題時，實際使用的範例吧。

Front desk　Thanks for calling the Front desk.
How many I help you?

Lora　Hi, I'm  **having slight hiccups** here. My bathroom sink isn't draining very well and the bedroom lights are flickering. I was wondering if I could get a room change.

Front desk　I'm terribly sorry about that. I'll take care of it right now.

Lora　Thank you. Could I get extra complimentary water bottles?

Front desk　Absolutely.

Lora　Also a kettle, please!

櫃檯　感謝您的來電，請問您需要什麼服務呢？

蘿拉　您好，我這裡有點小問題，我廁所的洗手台水流不太下去，還有床頭燈會閃。我在想是不是可以換房間。

櫃檯　真的非常抱歉，我馬上為您處理。

蘿拉　謝謝，那可以免費提供水給我嗎？

櫃檯　當然。

蘿拉　還有煮水壺，麻煩了！

MOST ASKED 「洗手台的水下不去！」、「馬桶沖不下去！」英文怎麼說？

去飯店難免會遇到水流不下去，以及各種問題，所以旅行前一定要知道這些話怎麼說。水流不下去時，可以說 The sink isn't draining. 或 Water won't go down the drain.。馬桶沖不下去，則可以說 The toilet isn't flushing. 或 The toilet is clogged.。

Don't flush wet wipes down the toilet.
請勿把濕紙巾丟進馬桶沖掉。

PATTERN I was wondering if ~

此句型可以用在有禮貌拜託某件事的時候，直譯為「我好奇是否能～」。be 動詞用過去式 was，聽起來較謙虛有禮，同樣的 Could I ~ 通常比 Can I ~ 聽起來更有禮貌，而 I was wondering if ~ 也比 May I ~ 更委婉。

Excuse me, I was wondering if I could get a refill. 不好意思，請問可以續杯嗎？	**I was wondering if I could get more salad dressing.** 是否能給我多一點沙拉醬呢？

EXPRESSION take care of (something)

大家都知道這個片語是「照顧」的意思，但是在辦公室、商業領域常當作「處理」的意思。

Who took care of this? 是誰處理這件事？	**Take care of this immediately!** 馬上處理這件事！

EXPRESSION complimentary

意為「免費的」，比 free 更常在飯店使用。如果不想花大錢喝水，一定要先確認水是否為 complimentary。amenities（備品）則是指飯店提供的洗髮精、沐浴乳等。

MOST ASKED 「熱水壺」英文怎麼說？

住飯店，房內用來煮水泡泡麵、咖啡的「熱水壺」稱為 kettle 或 electric kettle（電熱水壺）。

英文諺語 The pot calling the kettle black 直譯為鍋子笑水壺黑，意為「五十步笑百步」。Hello pot, meet kettle. 則是指對方「半斤八兩，還敢笑別人」。

Excuse my French
抱歉，我說了粗話

直譯為「請原諒我使用法文」，但其實 French 在此處是指髒話或不得體的語言。其起源於英法百年戰爭，因英國人與法國人不共戴天，視對方為眼中釘，因此英國人認為法國人粗魯又無禮，才會有此俚語。

這句話可以用在說髒話或不當發言之後或之前，代表「抱歉，我說了粗話」、「抱歉我講髒話」、「雖然我說的話可能不那麼中聽」等的意思。也可以說 Pardon my French. 或 Excuse my language.。在英語圈國家使用沒問題，只是在法國人面前使用可能有點沒禮貌，千萬要記得！

Mom	Give me your phone. Your phone is confiscated.
Son	What? Bullshit!
Mom	What did you just say? Watch your language!
Son	💬 **Excuse my French** but this isn't fair!
Mom	You are grounded for a week. Go upstairs!
Son	You can't do this to me, Mom!

媽媽	手機拿來，我要沒收。
兒子	什麼？太靠杯了！
媽媽	你剛剛說什麼？注意你的用詞！
兒子	抱歉，是我講話太超過，可是哪有人這樣的！
媽媽	接下來一個禮拜你不准出門，給我上去！
兒子	媽，妳不能這樣！

SLANG bullshit

牛屎？shit 雖然是「大便」的意思，但當作俚語來用更接近於髒話。這個字是「廢話」、「騙人」、「胡說八道」的意思，接近「我聽你在放屁」。常縮寫成 BS，也可以當動詞使用。

Stop bullshitting me!
別唬爛我了！

EXPRESSION Watch your language!

這裡的 watch 不是「看」，而是「小心」的意思，整句話的意思是「小心你的用詞！」，也可以省略 Watch your，只說 Language! 也可以。

MOST ASKED 「冤枉」正確的英文怎麼說？

fair 是「公平、公正」的意思，和 not 一起使用，則是「不公平」，即「冤枉」的意思。經常用在表達自己很委屈，帶有「哪有人這樣的！」、「這太扯了」的意思。

This is so not fair! I didn't do anything to deserve this.
這太扯了！憑什麼我要接受這種對待！

EXPRESSION grounded

美國青春電影中經常出現的用語就是「禁足」。grounded 是被綁在地上的意思，也可以當作「禁止飛行」的意思，在國高中生之間很常被當作「因為受罰，而無法出門和朋友見面」之意。

I'm sorry I can't go out tonight. I got grounded.
抱歉，我今晚不能出門，我被禁足了。

GRAMMAR 「go upstairs」的介系詞 to 去哪裡了？

upstairs 是名詞，意為「樓上」，但這裡是副詞，意思是「在樓上」、「往樓上」，不需要任何介系詞。台灣人最常犯的錯誤之一，就是在這個片語中加上介系詞 to，說成 go to upstairs。downstairs（往樓下）也是同樣的情況。

Come upstairs! I'm upstairs now.
上來！我現在在樓上。

Lose one's touch
寶刀已老

意為「失去原本出色的實力或手藝」。因此如果以否定來表達：You haven't lost your touch! 則是說你寶刀未老，還是一樣讚的意思。要小心不要和「失去聯絡」的 lose touch 搞混哦！為了不讓語言退步，也需要持續練習哦。別忘了，Practice makes perfect!（熟能生巧！）

Drew	I don't get chicks like I used to. I've totally **lost my touch**.
Alice	Your pick up lines are way too cheesy, yo.
Drew	"Did you get your license suspended for driving guys crazy?" What about it?
Alice	Eww, I got goosebumps.
Drew	Did it hurt? When you fell from heaven?
Alice	Stop!

德魯	我已經不像以前那樣會把妹了，我已經弱掉了。
愛麗絲	你那些撩妹的話都太油了，好嗎？
德魯	那這句如何？「妳的美太犯規，讓人想抱緊處理！」*
愛麗絲	噁耶，我都起雞皮疙瘩了。
德魯	妳會痛嗎？當妳從天堂掉下來的時候？
愛麗絲	夠了！

＊編按：此句撩妹話原文使用到雙關，drive 為「駕駛」之意，但也可用在片語 drive sb crazy，意指「驅使某人瘋狂」。因此原文整句直譯為「妳是否因讓男人瘋狂而被吊銷駕照了呢？」。

 **chick**

這個字有「小雞」的意思，也用來稱「女孩」或「女人」。男人很常用，聽起來不至於讓人感到不悅，不過還是會有人覺得刺耳，要小心使用。

Did you see that chick? She's hot.
你有看到那個小妞嗎？她超辣。

 「搭訕」英文怎麼說？

通常在路上遇到心儀的對象，過去攀談認識，正確的説法應該是 pick up sb 或 hit on sb，而搭訕台詞則是 pick-up line。而「與某人調情」則可説 flirt with sb。

He always tries to pick up girls at bars.
他每次都要在酒吧把妹。

MOST ASKED 人很「油條」正確的英文怎麼說？

oily 或 greasy 是「油膩的」，指吃起來很油、很膩的食物，不會拿來形容人。其實英文沒有完全契合的替換字，因為美國人文化上本來就比較擅長社交。cheesy 本來有點「不悦」、「廉價」的意思，但是也有「在愛情方面，過於情緒化、而且太過肉麻又幼稚」的意思。

I want to do cheesy things with my boyfriend like wearing matching outfits.
我想和我男友做些肉麻幼稚的事，像是穿情侶裝。

EXCLAMATION yo

用在歡迎對方、叫喚對方、想引起關注或表現興奮之情時，當作感嘆詞使用，類似中文的「嘿」、「哇」。

Yo, that's awesome. | **Hey, yo!**
哇，那太讚了。 | 嘿！

MOST ASKED 「起雞皮疙瘩」英文怎麼說？

「雞皮疙瘩」如果直譯成 chicken skin 是不對的！正確的説法是 goosebumps，可以用在感覺肉麻而「起雞皮疙瘩」的時候。

She's got a heavenly voice. It gives me goosebumps when she sings.
她天生好歌喉，聽她唱歌的時候，我都起雞皮疙瘩了。

Throw someone under the bus
背叛

把某人丟到公車下？雖然很驚悚，但事實上並非如此，這個用法的意思是為了一己私利背叛或犧牲他人；當自己處於困境時，反而怪罪他人、懲罰他人的意思，經常使用在孩子們為了不受罰而彼此推卸責任時。

Jennifer Did you tell the boss that I misinformed you the date of the meeting?

Dylan Yeah. You said the meeting has been postponed.

Jennifer I never said that! You are putting words in my mouth.

Dylan Why are you so angry?

Jennifer Because you are trying to 💬 **throw me under the bus**. You are twisting my words!

Dylan I'm sorry but that's exactly what you said.

珍妮佛 你是不是跟老闆說，我跟你說錯開會時間？

迪倫 嗯，妳說會議被延後啊。

珍妮佛 我才不是那樣說的！你亂講。

迪倫 妳幹嘛這麼怒？

珍妮佛 因為你就是想搞我啊。你根本亂傳達我說的話！

迪倫 不好意思，可是妳的確是那樣說的啊。

MOST CONFUSED postpone vs. delay

字典上兩者都有「推遲」、「延後」的意思，但是有時候用起來的語感不同。delay 大部分是因為出乎意料的自然災害或特定狀況，不得已才將時間延後的意思；但是 postpone 指事先計劃的活動或會議被改到之後的另外一天。

The meeting is delayed.
會議延後開始。

＊當天有突發狀況，延後開始。

The meeting is postponed.
會議改期了。

＊已預期變故，改到其他日期。

My flight got delayed due to heavy snow.
我的班機因為大雪而延遲。

＊因為自然災害，導致班機延後。

PATTERN I've never + Vp.p.（過去分詞）

這是母語人士每天必用的句型，意為「我從未～」。原本的說法為 I have never，但是口語會省略 have，只說 I never。

I've never tried stinky tofu.
我沒吃過臭豆腐。

I've never been to Germany.
我沒去過德國。

IDIOM put words in my mouth

把言論強塞到某人嘴裡，指「曲解或誤會對方所說的意思」，也可以解釋為「捏造他人從未說過的言論」。

Don't put words in my mouth. I've never said that!
你不要在那裡造謠，我沒說過那種話！

EXPRESSION twist one's words

twist 有「扭、轉」及「轉折」等各種意思，但是也有「扭曲」事實的意思，因此這個片語的意思就是「曲解某人的話」或「短章取義」。而 twist fact/truth 則是扭曲事實。

Sometimes the media twists facts.
媒體偶爾會扭曲事實。

Wear one's heart on one's sleeve
把心情寫在臉上

指不會隱藏或壓抑自己的情緒或想法，直接表達出來的意思。如果「把心臟掏出來當袖子穿」，把情緒完整暴露在自己的行為或話語中，旁邊的人怎麼可能不知道，尤其常用來表現「藏不住心中的喜愛之情」。

Colon	Lighten up!
Sarah	Everything here is not hunky-dory.
Colon	I know but you can't 💬 **wear your heart on your sleeve** all the time. You are making everyone feel uncomfy.
Sarah	But I can't help it.
Colon	You need to learn how to discipline and contain your emotions. I've wanted to get this off my chest for a long time.

科隆	放輕鬆！
莎拉	這裡的一切都很不 OK！
科隆	我知道，但是妳不能每次都把心情寫在臉上，妳這樣會讓大家不舒服。
莎拉	但我就控制不了啊。
科隆	我老早就想跟妳說，妳需要學會控制和了解妳自己的情緒。

EXPRESSION **lighten up**

雖然有使用更亮的顏色提高色調的意思，但是當作命令句時，是叫對方不要太憂鬱和凝重，可以當作「振作起來」、「笑一個」、「加油」、「別氣了」等意思使用。

I want to lighten up my hair a bit.
我想把髮色弄亮一點。

A glass of wine lightens up my mood.
一杯紅酒能夠紓緩我的情緒。

SLANG **hunky-dory**

指活動或情況如自己所願、符合自己期待，令人感到滿意且無可挑剔的意思，也可以用在心情很好的時候。

All the kids were hunky-dory playing with new toys.
所有孩子都很滿足地玩新玩具。

Today's important meeting was hunky-dory and our boss is very pleased.
今天的重要會議一切順利，而且我們老闆非常開心。

SPOKEN ENGLISH **uncomfy**

uncomfortable（不舒服）的口語縮寫，comfortable（舒服）則縮寫成 comfy。

EXPRESSION **I can't help it**

「無可奈何、無能為力、情不自禁」的意思，用在情況無奈，或像會話內容中，用於無法控制自己的時候。〈I can't help ＋動名詞〉則可以表達「不得不～」。

I can't help loving you because you are so lovable.
我不得不愛你，因為你真的太可愛了。

IDIOM **get (something) off one's chest**

長期放在心裡的事能夠一吐為快，包括傾訴自己的煩惱，或坦白地承認自己的錯誤。

Let's get things off our chests and talk about what's been bothering.
讓我們彼此坦誠自己的內心，談談困擾我們的問題。

Hit the sack
去睡覺

sack 是「麻袋」的意思，因為以前的人會把堆滿麻袋的乾草，當作床或枕頭來睡覺，所以這個慣用語就是指「上床睡覺」的意思。類似的說法還有 hit the hay。

Erica	I'm gonna 💬 **hit the sack** now.
Marc	It's 9 right now.
Erica	I've got a big day ahead of me tomorrow.
	I've gotta get my beauty sleep.
Marc	Whatever it is, crossing my fingers for you.
Erica	Thank you. Nighty night.
Marc	Don't let the bed bugs bite. Sweet dreams.

埃莉卡	我現在要去睡了。
馬克	現在才九點。
埃莉卡	明天是個大日子，我必須睡個美容覺。
馬克	不管是什麼事，我祝妳好運。
埃莉卡	謝啦，晚安。
馬克	祝妳一夜好眠，有個美夢。

EXPRESSION I've got a big day ahead of me.

這裡的 big 不是指大小的「大」，而是「重要」的意思。big day 可以是面試、婚禮、第一天上班等因人而異的事。

We've got a big day ahead of us tomorrow! I hope our meeting goes well.
明天是我們的大日子！希望我們會議順利！

IDIOM beauty sleep

這個詞彙來自《睡美人》，也就是睡飽七～九小時。因為晚上十二點前睡覺，睡眠才會充足，皮膚才會變好、變健康，看起來也才不會有疲倦感。

You couldn't get your beauty sleep last night, huh?
You have dark circles under your eyes.
你昨晚沒睡飽對吧？你眼下有黑眼圈耶。

EXPRESSION nighty night

good night 的可愛說法，nighty night 小孩子比較常用，但是對任何人都可以用溫柔的語氣說。

Nighty night. Sleep tight.
晚安，祝你好眠。

IDIOM Don't let the bed bugs bite.

直譯就是「小心別被床上的蟲子咬」。相信大家都有夏天睡覺時，凌晨被蚊子咬醒的經驗，所以這句話就是「不要被吵醒，睡沉一點」的意思。家長唱給孩子們聽的歌曲，就有句「Good night, sleep tight, don't let the bed bugs bite.」，也常直接使用在會話上。

See you in the morning, sweetie. Don't let the bed bugs bite.
寶貝，早上見囉。一夜好眠。

EXPRESSION Sweet dreams.

「祝你有個美夢」的意思，就是希望對方不要做惡夢，睡個好覺。

A: Sweet dreams. 晚安。

B: Sweet dreams to you, too. 你也晚安哦。

Get one's ducks in a row
做好萬全準備

不覺得排成一列的鴨子給人一種整齊又做好準備的感覺嗎？因此就是用來表達「為了計畫，連小事都徹頭徹尾地準備」，也有「為了日後可能會發生的事做好萬般的準備」。

Son	The turkey smells finger licking good! Where is the cranberry sauce by the way?
Mom	It is in the fridge. Can you put this gravy on the table, too?
Son	Wow, Mom! You've really 💬 **got your ducks in a row** for this Thanksgiving!
Mom	Let's say the grace and dig in, everybody.
Son	May God bless us and everyone around us. Amen!
Mom	Hope you all enjoy the food!

兒子	烤火雞聞起來也太香了吧！話說蔓越莓醬在哪裡？
媽媽	在冰箱。你可以順便把這碗肉醬擺到桌上去嗎？
兒子	哇！媽，妳真的為感恩節做好萬全準備耶！
媽媽	讓我們先來禱告再開動吧，大家。
兒子	願主保佑我們和我們身邊所有的人，阿門！
媽媽	希望你們好好享用今天的食物！

EXPRESSION **finger licking good**

「好吃到吮指」的意思，也是 KFC 肯德基長久以來的廣告標語。

This fried chicken is finger licking good!
這炸雞太好吃了！

CULTURE **cranberry sauce, gravy**

講到「感恩節」就會想到烤火雞，而蔓越莓醬（cranberry sauce）和肉汁（gravy）則是烤火雞不可或缺的醬料。推薦大家一定要嚐一次這個組合，就算搜圖來看流流口水也好！

CULTURE **say the grace**

這是美國感恩節的文化，一家人會圍坐餐桌，抓著彼此的手，對這一年來接受的恩惠表示感恩和祈禱。「祈禱」的英文有 say the grace、say a prayer、pray 等各種不同的說法。

MOST ASKED **「開動吧！」正確的英文怎麼說？**

宴客主邀請大家「開動吧」，可以說 Let's eat.，比較日常的說法是 Let's dig in.。賓客要開動時，可以說 Thank you!，感謝對方款待。

A: Let's dig in. 開動吧！
B: Thank you so much for the food you made! 謝謝你做的所有食物！

MOST MISTAKEN **「用餐愉快！」正確的英文怎麼說？**

祝別人用餐愉快，絕對不是 Eat happily.。正確的說法很簡單，就是 Enjoy your food! / Enjoy your meal! / Hope you enjoy! 等，或法文的 Bon appétit!，美國人也很常用。

A: Did you enjoy the food? 有吃飽嗎？
B: Yes, I totally loved it! Thank you! 有，我吃得很開心！謝謝！

Let's Practice!
DAY 81-90

Exercise 1 請用題目中給的單字造句。

1. 我有點小麻煩。（slight）

_____

2. 我完全聽不懂。（Greek）

_____

3. 這不公平。（This isn't）

_____

4. 我寶刀已老。（my）

_____

5. 你亂講我說的話。（in my mouth）

_____

6. 你是在弄我。（under the bus）

_____

7. 我藏不住情緒。（I wear）

_____

8. 我要去睡了。（the sack）

_____

9. 你身材看起來很結實。（toned）

_____

10. 我起雞皮疙瘩了。（I got）

_____

解答 1

1) I'm having slight hiccups.   2) It's (all) Greek to me.   3) This isn't fair.   4) I lost my touch.
5) You are putting words in my mouth.   6) You are trying to throw me under the bus.
7) I wear my heart on my sleeve.   8) I'm gonna hit the sack.   9) You look very toned.
10) I got goosebumps.

1. 抱歉，我說了粗話。

Excuse my _____.

2. 別理他！

_____ it off!

3. 我必須做好萬全準備。

I need to get _____.

4. 免費提供的水

_____ water bottles

5. 絕對不可能有那種事。

_____ fly.

6. 放屁！

_____ shit!

7. 就笑笑帶過吧！

Let's _____.

8. 搖擺州

_____ state

9. 振作起來吧。

_____ up.

10. 冷靜點。

C_____.

解答 2

1) French　2) Brush　3) my ducks in a row　4) Complimentary　5) When pigs　6) Bull
7) laugh it off　8) Swing　9) Lighten　10) Chillax

Get to the bottom of it
追根究底

揭發某事發生的理由，即「追根究底」的意思。除了有透過調查把背後的原因找出來的意思之外，也可以用來表達找到解決問題的方法，相同的片語還有 lie/be at the bottom，因為這個片語有「在底部」的意思，所以也有找到根本原因的意思。

Mary	Sarah said she will sue Melissa for spreading malicious rumors about her.
Carl	You can't be serious!
Mary	Isn't Melissa infamous for having a big mouth?
Carl	No way! The Melissa I know is not that type of a person.
Mary	Why are you taking her side?
Carl	I really need to 💬 **get to the bottom of what happened**. Something is very wrong!

瑪莉	莎拉說她會告梅麗莎誹謗她。
卡爾	妳認真？
瑪莉	梅麗莎不是出了名的大嘴巴嗎？
卡爾	不可能！我認識的梅麗莎不是這種人。
瑪莉	你為什麼站在她那邊？
卡爾	我必須搞清楚發生什麼事，我覺得不對勁！

CULTURE

sue 是「提告」的意思，也可以說 file a lawsuit（提起訴訟）。美國可以說是「告到底」（告到底）的國家，有很多超乎我們想像的情況都能打官司，像潛艇堡連鎖店「Subway」就曾經因為潛艇堡長度和廣告差 1 英吋就被告了。I'll sue you.（我要告你。）這話很常聽到，因為美國人很重視自己的權利，無法忍受自己權利受損。

I filed a lawsuit against the company.
我會向公司提出告訴。

EXPRESSION **You can't be serious!**

覺得對方說的話不可置信時就可以說這句話，意為「你不是認真的吧、太扯了、不可能」，類似的說法還有 You've got to be kidding me.（你一定是在跟我開玩笑。）。

A: OMG! I've won a lottery! 天啊！我中樂透了！
B: You can't be serious! 太扯了！

MOST CONFUSED **famous vs. infamous**

這兩個字都是「有名」的意思，只是 famous 是正面的有名，infamous 則是負面的「惡名昭彰」。

MOST ASKED **「大嘴巴」正確的英文怎麼說？**

可以說 have a big mouth，也可以說 can't keep a secret。big mouth 就是指「大嘴巴的人、話多的人」。

Nancy has a big mouth. She really can't keep a secret.
南希真的很大嘴巴，她守不住秘密。

EXPRESSION **take one's side**

在起口角或不合的狀況下，「偏袒某人」或「站在某一方」的意思。

I'm not taking anyone's side.
我不會偏袒任何人。

She never takes sides. She always stays neutral.
她絕對不會選邊站，她總是保持中立。

Beggars can't be choosers
吃人嘴軟，拿人手短

乞丐沒有選擇的餘地，也就是「要飯的哪能挑肥揀瘦」、「感激不盡」、「哪能選喜歡還是討厭」等意思，沒有選擇權的時候，即使不符預期，也要懂得知足的語感。choosing beggars 則是相反的意思，指「用很差的條件提出誇張要求的人」。

Sydney　Do you think I can borrow your pickup truck tomorrow?

Hose　Are you going shopping for Black Friday?

Sydney　Yeah, I'm going to get that 75-inch TV.
I wanted to bring it home myself.

Hose　I haven't washed my car for a while though.
It might stink inside.

Sydney　💬 **Beggars can't be choosers.** I will fill up the gas tank for you.

Hose　Fantabulous!

辛妮　明天我可以跟你借皮卡車嗎？

豪斯　妳是黑色星期五要去掃貨嗎？

辛妮　嗯，我要去買 75 吋的電視，我想自己搬回家。

豪斯　我有段時間沒洗車了說，裡面應該很臭。

辛妮　你願意借我就偷笑了，我會幫你加滿油的。

豪斯　太棒了！

CULTURE **pickup trucks**

在美國，卡車除了用在搬運貨品，只要自己喜歡也可以擁有。pickup truck（皮卡車）是美國人最喜歡的車款之一，也是一種美國文化。在加州可以看到，大部分喜歡露營或衝浪的男性，都會把皮卡車改裝得很帥。

CULTURE **Black Friday**

11 月的第四個星期四是 Thanksgiving（感恩節），隔天就是 Black Friday（黑色星期五）。這天是美國一年中，商場折扣最多的期間，也是大家開始正式採購聖誕節用品的時候。網路上可以輕易找到每當這時候很多人從凌晨就開始排隊，甚至為了爭奪想買的物品大動干戈的影片。

近幾年則是開始流行起 Cyber Monday（網購星期一），時間就在黑色星期五後的第一個星期一，在這天則是輪到各家電商推出大規模促銷活動，類似於我們的雙 11 網購節。

EXPRESSION **oneself**

就像會話中的用法，強調「一個人親自」時可以用，也有平常「自己真正的樣子」的意思。

Did you make this yourself?
這是你自己做的嗎？

I'm just going to be myself.
我要做自己。

EXPRESSION **stink**

雖然 smell 是「發出味道」的意思，但是 stink 是「發出惡臭」，在味道的強度上有不同的意義。這個字也類似 sucks，覺得某個事物很不怎麼樣時，可以用來表達「厭惡」的意思。

That movie stinks. Don't bother watching it.
那部電影太糟了，真的不用花時間看了。

Your feet are stinking up the whole room.
整間房間都是你的腳臭味。

SLANG **fantabulous**

這個字是 fantastic 和 fabulous 的合成語，是「很優秀、超棒」的意思。如果使用 fabulous 還不夠，就可以使用這個字。

Your Thanksgiving dinner was fantabulous! You really outdid yourself.
你的感恩節晚餐真的太讚了！比你平常做得更好吃。

Think outside the box
跳脫思考框架

墨西哥玉米捲餅店「Tacobell」（塔可鐘）的標語是「Think outside the bun」，背後的意思就是要大家脫離漢堡，改嘗試新的東西，也就是 Tacobell 的捲餅。這個慣用語的意思就是「跳脫固定框架，從創新角度思考，挑戰新事物」，包含了打開新視角、打破框架、學習新事物、邁向從未走過的道路等面向。

Ray I'm having second thoughts about taking a year off and traveling.

Lora Why? Are you scared of getting out of your comfort zone?

Ray I'm also afraid that I might not be able to get a job right after I graduate.

Lora You don't have to get a job right away.
💬 **Think outside the box**.

Ray True.

Lora You should get out there and expand your horizon.

雷　　我在遲疑是不是真的要休學一年去旅行。
蘿拉　為什麼？你害怕脫離舒適圈嗎？
雷　　我也害怕我畢業之後無法馬上找到工作。
蘿拉　你不必馬上找到工作啊，跳脫這種舊思維。
雷　　也是。
蘿拉　你應該走出去拓展你的視野。

EXPRESSION **have second thoughts**

意為在決定做某事後，因為擔心、懷疑、不安、愧疚感等原因而再次考慮。可以用在擔心且遲疑猶豫的時候。

Are you having second thoughts about your marriage?
你在猶豫結婚的事嗎？

I had no second thoughts about it at all.
我對那件事毫無懸念。

MOST ASKED **「休學」、「休假」正確的英文怎麼說？**

「上班」是 go to work，「休學」和「休假」可以使用 take/have ~ off，動詞後面可以和幾天、幾年等休息時間連用。若在學校犯錯被強制休學，則用 suspend (someone) from school。

I took a semester off last year.
我去年請一學期的假。

I have a day off today.
我今天請一天假。

I'm going to take this Friday off.
我這週五要請假。

EXPRESSION **get out of one's comfort zone**

脫離舒適圈？就是指擺脫日常生活中習慣的事物。例如不安於舒適又安定的日常，改變重複的日常生活，和新的人見面、挑戰新事物、嘗試不曾做過的事等等。

Get out of your comfort zone and you will see yourself grow.
脫離舒適圈，然後你會看到自己的成長。

IDIOM **expand one's horizon**

「拓寬自己的地平線」意為親自嘗試各種不同的新體驗以拓展自己的視野。此刻我們正認真學習英語也算在其中哦！

A: I have never traveled abroad. 我從未去國外旅行過。

B: Really? At your age, you really need to broaden your horizon.
真的嗎？以你的年紀來說，真的該去拓寬一下你的視野。

Born with a silver spoon in one's mouth

含著金湯匙出生

雖然我們說出生和成長背景富裕的人是「含金湯匙」，但是美國是說「含銀湯匙」。這個俚語的由來，是源自以前英國在為嬰兒洗禮時，貴族都會送給小孩銀湯匙。貴族就是上流階層，等同於父母的社會地位高。相反地，「土湯匙」可以說 wooden spoon，不過這個詞比較少用。

Adam   John seems to be super loaded.

Lora   He was actually  **born with a silver spoon in his mouth**. His father is filthy rich.

Adam   Come to think of it, he is the biggest spender I've met.

Lora   But he's had a part-time job for a long time and he never brags about what he has.

Adam   I know!

Lora   That is why everyone loves him.

亞當   約翰好像超有錢。

蘿拉   其實他家很有錢，他爸是土豪耶。

亞當   這樣想起來，他是我見過花錢最大手筆的人耶。

蘿拉   可是他打工打很久了，而且從來沒吹噓他擁有什麼。

亞當   就是啊！

蘿拉   這也是為什麼大家這麼愛他啊。

IDIOM come to think of it

「仔細想想」、「這樣想起來」的意思，可以用在説話時突然想起某事、有個想法或有所領悟的時候。

Come to think of it, I don't think I locked my car.
突然想想，我好像沒鎖車。

Now I come to think of it, I think I also need to apologize.
現在想起來，我覺得我也應該要道歉。

EXPRESSION big spender

指「花錢大手筆的人」，根據情境和文章脈絡，也可以用在負面如「揮霍無度」的情況。

MOST ASKED 「打工」怎麼說？

打工的意思，即「兼職工作」，正確的説法是 part-time job，打工仔則是 part-timer。

I currently work as a part-timer at a restaurant.
我現在在餐廳打工。

EXPRESSION brag

「炫耀自負」的意思，偶爾也可以用來表達極度 flex（愛誇耀的）。類似的説法還有 boast 跟 show off。

One's mind is in the gutter
心術不正

gutter 是「排水溝」，因此也衍伸為「低俗」、「低級」等意思，通常是形容思想「低級」、「色色的」的意思。我們會説愛開黃腔或思想不純正的人是變態，英文就可以用這句話哦。

Stephanie　I had a blast last night chatting up Terry. We pulled an all-nighter.

Eddie　Did you guys make out?

Stephanie　What? No! 💬 **Your mind is in the gutter!**

Eddie　Well, what do you like about him?

Stephanie　He speaks his mind. He is very vocal.

Eddie　It seems like he is gonna be the one who wears the pants in this relationship!

史蒂芬妮　我昨晚和泰迪聊得很開心，我們聊了一整夜。

艾迪　你們有沒有做色色的事？

史蒂芬妮　什麼？沒有啦！你很低級耶！

艾迪　好啦，那妳喜歡他什麼？

史蒂芬妮　他很懂得説出自己的想法，很直言不諱。

艾迪　看來這段關係，主導權都會在他手上哦。

IDIOM have a blast

和 have a lot of fun 是一樣的意思，用來表達「真的過得很愉快」、「太有趣了」。

I hope you have a blast at your senior prom!
希望你高中舞會玩得開心！

IDIOM pull an all-nighter

為了熬夜做什麼而「整晚沒睡」。大部分用在為了唸書或工作而熬夜，但這不是鐵則，也可用在為了專注於做某事而熬夜。

I pulled an all-nighter procrastinating for the test today.
為了今天的考試，我熬夜臨時抱佛腳。

IDIOM make out

口語中指接吻、上床等親密的肢體接觸。一般的肢體接觸，可以説 get physical、 physical contact 或委婉的 physical affection（肉體之愛）等。

I don't like to get physical until I really know the person.
在我真正認識一個人之前，我不喜歡有肢體接觸。

Let's not get physical here! No violence!
這裡不允許任何肢體衝突！禁止暴力！

IDIOM speak one's mind

坦白地説出自己的想法和感覺的意思，依情境也可以用來形容講話直接、該説什麼就説什麼的個性。

Can you just speak your mind? I promise I won't get upset.
你可以老實説出你的想法嗎？我答應你我不生氣。

IDIOM wear the pants

在戀人關係中或家中，扮演主宰者或手握主權的意思。雖然過去是用來形容「態度強勢的女人」，但是現在形容男人或女人皆可。

Who wears the pants in your relationship?
你們之間誰是作主的那個？

219

Have a lot on one's plate
忙得不可開交

「盤子上堆很多東西」就是工作很多，要解決很多問題的意思，當業務或各種事物堆積如山，忙得不可開交時，就可以使用這句話。因此，可以拿來說「要煩的事很多」、「很忙」、「忙得暈頭轉向」。

Tyler　I 💬 **have a lot on my plate**. It's not even funny.

Lora　You are really living your life the fullest these days.

Tyler　I am, but I haven't had any quality time with my parents for a while.

Lora　No matter what you gotta make some time. They won't be there forever.

Tyler　Right. Time is limited for all of us. I always forget that.

Lora　I know it's easier said than done but call them up and say I love you!

泰勒　我要忙死了，沒在開玩笑的。

蘿拉　你這陣子過得真充實。

泰勒　我是啊，可是我卻無法抽出一點時間陪我爸媽。

蘿拉　無論如何你還是得抽點空，他們不會永遠都在。

泰勒　沒錯，所有人的時間都是有限的，我總是忘記這點。

蘿拉　我知道說比做容易，但你還是打給他們說我愛你們吧！

EXPRESSION It's not (even) funny.

雖然如字面上是「無趣且不好笑」的意思，但是可以當作「不是開玩笑的」、「很驚人」、「奇怪」、「太氣人了」、「很嚴重」等各種意思。

Why are you laughing at his joke? It's not funny.
你怎麼會被他的笑話逗笑？一點都不好笑。

It is freezing outside. It's not even funny!
外面真的超冷的，不是開玩笑的！

IDOM live one's life the fullest

「將生活活到最滿」也就是說不安於現況，盡可能使用現在被賦予的一切，去執行各種體驗，過得充實的意思。Live your life the fullest! YOLO (You Only Live Once)！

My father never stops learning and trying new things. He truly lives his life the fullest.
我爸從未停止學習和嘗試新事物，他真的把自己的人生過得很充實。

EXPRESION quality time

意為「珍貴且有意義的時間」，尤指和親近的家人朋友度過有意義的時光。

I spent some quality time with my dad on his birthday.
在爸爸生日這天，我和他一起度過珍貴且有意義的時光。

EXPRESSION make (some) time

「製造時間」，即「空出時間」的意思。

Thank you for making the time.
謝謝你抽空。

Can you make some time for me on Saturday?
星期六你可以為我空下來嗎？

IDOM It's easier said than done.

「說起來簡單」或「做的不像說的簡單」的意思。雖然從理論來看或用想的，會覺得簡單，但是真的付諸行動卻感到困難。

Studying English every day is easier said than done.
每天念英文，真是說的比做的容易。

Put oneself in someone else's shoes

設身處地為人著想

為了瞭解對方的立場，與他感同身受，而「換位思考」的意思。意思就是，藉由穿他人的鞋子，來思考那個人的想法，以及間接體驗他的狀況。

Beth　With all due respect, you were a bit rude to the waiter.

Max　Was I? I could be a little fussy from time to time.

Beth　Well, 💬 **put yourself in his shoes**. It might have ruined his day.

Max　Oh...

Beth　Everyone is fighting their own battle we don't know. So we need to be kind.

Max　Wow. It is really something to think about. Thanks.

貝絲　恕我直言，你剛剛對服務生有點沒禮貌。

麥克斯　我有嗎？我有時候真的有點難搞。

貝絲　嗯，你也換位思考一下吧。這有可能會毀了他的一天。

麥克斯　喔……

貝絲　每個人都有我們不知道的奮鬥要面對，所以我們應該對人友善一點。

麥克斯　哇，這值得深思，謝啦。

EXPRESSION **with all due respect**

當打算責怪對方或不認同對方時，鄭重表達自己的想法之前，希望對方聽了不要不開心，等同於「恕我直言」、「這些話説來冒昧」等正式説法一樣，不過根據情境也可以對朋友使用，畢竟越熟就越要尊敬對方！

With all due respect, I disagree with your opinion.
恕我直言，我不同意你説的話。

With all due respect sir, I think you should look at the bigger picture.
恕我直言，但您必須縱觀全局。

EXPRESSION **fussy**

意指「挑剔又敏感」，也有小題大作或要求超多的意思。

Kyle is a fussy eater. It is very hard to satisfy him.
凱爾真的嘴很挑，超難滿足他的。

EXPRESSION **from time to time**

「偶爾」、「時不時」的意思，可以用這個片語取代老派的 sometimes。類似的説法還有 once in a while、now and then、occasionally 等。

I miss what we had from time to time.
有時候我會想念我們在一起的時光。

From time to time, I go to the drive-in movie theater.
我偶爾會去露天停車戲院。

EXPRESSION **something**

雖然我們知道這個字是「某種東西」，但 something 也可以指某人事物「重要、了不起、有料的」等意思。

Don't forget. You are something!
別忘了，你很特別！

He is definitely something. I know he will be famous someday.
他的確有三兩三，我知道總有一天他一定會紅！

Get the hang of it
抓到訣竅

指學習做某事的必備技能，開始理解後，漸漸熟悉、上手的意思。例如當開始熟悉開車、用電腦、滑雪、打高爾夫球等事之後，我們就會說「抓到訣竅了」、「我現在稍微知道怎麼做了」、「我掌握要領了」。

Mom　Are you still working on your math homework?

Son　Yeah. It's a tough nut to crack.

Mom　Once you 💬 **get the hang of it**, it'll become a piece of cake for you.

Son　Ah! I just wanna get it over with and watch TV!

Mom　If you can't focus why don't you freshen up and go back to it?

Son　That would work!

媽媽　你還在寫你的數學作業嗎？

兒子　對啊，這很難寫。

媽媽　當你抓到訣竅，對你來說就是小菜一碟了。

兒子　啊！我想快點寫完去看電視！

媽媽　如果你無法專注，要不要先去洗個澡再回來寫啊？

兒子　不錯耶！

IDIOM tough nut to crack

如字面上所示，一顆又硬又難敲開的核桃，意思就是在說「難搞的人」或「難以解決的問題」。

My boss is such a tough nut to crack. It is so hard to satisfy him.
我老闆很難搞，你很難滿足他。

COVID-19 is the hardest nut to crack for everyone across the world.
新冠肺炎對全世界來說是道難題。

IDIOM a piece of cake

這個慣用語大家應該都知道，就是「簡單」、「輕而易舉」的意思，類似的說法還有 easy peasy、no brainer 等。請注意 no brainer 是指簡單的事，不是罵人無腦唷。

A: How was the test? 你考得怎麼樣？

B: It was a piece of cake. No brainer! 很簡單，根本不用動腦！

With self-driving cars driving will be a piece of cake.
如果開自動駕駛汽車，開車就很簡單了。

EXPRESSION just wanna get it over with

「只想想快點解決」的意思，不想再思考，想快點解決才覺得痛快的語感。

I've been working on this project for 3 months.

I just wanna get it over with.
這個專案我已經做了三個月，我只想快點搞定它。

Let's just get it over with and have dinner.
讓我們快點解決，然後吃晚餐吧。

EXPRESSION freshen up

一般人想到「洗」只知道 wash 或 shower，下次不妨像母語人士一樣使用這個片語吧。這種「洗」是指為了讓心情變舒爽，而換衣服、梳頭髮並補妝、漱口等行為。

Make sure to freshen up right before the interview.
面試前一定要確定自己都整裝完畢了。

My flight was over 10 hours. I really want to freshen up.
我飛超過十小時，我真想洗個澡。

Sleep on it
考慮看看

意指不要倉促下決定，花點時間考慮看看。sleep 雖然是睡覺的意思，但這個片語的意思是至少花一個晚上的時間「仔細思考」。可以用在遇到難以馬上決定的問題，或需要深思熟慮的情況下。

CEO You know our new branch in Florida? Cut to the chase they need you there.

Gemma You really caught me off guard.

CEO Well, 💬 **sleep on it** and let me know by the end of this week.

Gemma Actually, I'll be more than happy to take the opportunity.

CEO Really?

Gemma You can count on me for the Florida branch. I won't let you down.

CEO 妳知道我們在佛羅里達的新分公司吧？我就直截了當地說了，我希望妳能過去。

潔瑪 你真的讓我措手不及。

CEO 嗯，妳好好考慮，這週結束前讓我知道。

潔瑪 其實我很樂意接受這個機會。

CEO 真的？

潔瑪 你可以放心把佛羅里達分公司交給我，我不會讓你失望。

IDIOM **cut to the chase**

單刀直入、開門見山,只講重點的意思。

I'm going to cut to the chase and ask you if you like me or not.
我就直接了當地問了,你喜不喜歡我?

Let's cut to the chase and talk about sales. How much did we make this month?
我們直接來談銷售量吧,這個月的銷售如何?

IDIOM **catch someone off guard**

「以無防備(off guard)之姿被抓到」意指因為意想不到的事情,而感到慌張或不知所措,也意指一時大意,被戳中要害。也可以用在像會話一樣,當遇到意想不到的提案或問題而感到慌張時,就可以使用。

I was caught off guard when Jenny showed up at my door step without any notice.
珍妮什麼都沒說就出現在我門前,嚇壞我了。

MOST CONFUSED **by vs. until**

兩個都有「~為止」的意思,但是語感稍微不同。by 把重點放在「no later than 某個時間點」,而 until 則是把重點擺在「在截止時間之前的所有時間」。

I need it by tonight.
今晚我就要。(不能過了今晚!今晚一定要給我。)

I need it until tonight.
到今晚我都需要。(從此刻到今晚都需要。)

I'll be there by 7.
我最晚七點到。(再晚不會超過七點。)

I'll be there until 7.
我會待到七點。(一直到七點為止都會待在那裡。)

EXPRESSION **count on (someone)**

意指在特別困難的狀況下依賴某人,並對其有所期望。大家可以聽聽「火星人布魯諾」(Bruno Mars)的〈Count On Me〉哦!

Everyone is counting on Tai Tzu-Ying to show the world what she's got.
所有人都在期待戴資穎讓全世界看到她的能耐。

EXPRESSION **let someone down**

指無論是否故意,無法遵守約定或無法達到期待,讓對方失望的意思。

You'd better not let me down again.
你最好不要再讓我失望。

227

Well begun is half done
好的開始是成功的一半

直譯即「好的開始，事情就能完成大半」，也就是付出心血，鼓起勇氣開始實踐某件事，就已經成功一半的意思；也有只要開始，就能順利結束的意思。也就是說，要開始一個新的挑戰真的不簡單，但是只要能讓自己的生活更豐富，那麼就一定要開始哦！

Bryce   It might be too late but I started learning English.

Rosalie You don't say! You hated English!

Bryce   It was the last thing on my mind but now my dream is to travel all around the world.

Rosalie Stop playing!

Bryce   It was a slap in the face when I got made fun of by my kids.

Rosalie That's OK! 💬 **Well begun is half done!**

布萊斯　或許有點太晚，不過我開始學英語了。
羅莎莉　不會吧！你不是討厭英語嗎？
布萊斯　雖然我之前不在意，但是現在我的夢想是環遊世界。
羅莎莉　少開玩笑了！
布萊斯　當我被我孩子嘲笑，真的很羞恥耶。
羅莎莉　沒關係！好的開始是成功的一半！

EXPRESSION **You don't say!**

像「不會吧！」、「太扯了！」這些句子一樣，表示驚訝和難以置信。而且當對方再講一件理所當然的事時，也可以用挖苦的語氣説。

A: Did you know Jeju is an island?
你知道濟州是座島嗎？

B: You don't say?
你認真？（當我白癡嗎？）

EXPRESSION **the last thing on my mind**

最後才想到的事情，當然不重要或不在考慮的範圍內。也就是指沒在想的事、最不喜歡的事或是不想做的事等。

Getting married is the last thing on my mind right now.
結婚是我目前最不考慮的事。

We broke up and now he is the last thing on my mind.
我們分手了，現在他對我來説是最不重要的人。

MOST ASKED **「環遊世界」正確的英文怎麼說？**

「環遊世界」的英語是 travel all around the world 或 travel the whole world。我相信，環遊世界能夠拓展自己的視野，觀察不一樣的生活方式。

EXPRESSION **stop playing**

可以像會話一樣當作「少騙了」的意思。也可以當作 stop playing (games)，「不要玩弄別人的心」的意思。

Stop playing games with my heart!
不要再玩弄我的心了！

IDIOM **a slap in the face**

想想看你突然被賞了一巴掌會怎樣？是不是驚訝、屈辱、憤怒等情緒一下子衝上腦門，而這個片語就是指能夠引發這所有情緒的事。

Not being promoted this year was a real slap in the face for me.
今年沒升職對我來説真的是莫大的屈辱。

Let's Practice!
DAY 91-100

Exercise 1　請用題目中給的單字造句。

1. 開拓你的視野。（horizon）

___

2. 你這變態！（Your mind）

___

3. 我度過很開心的時光。（blast）

___

4. 珍妮是含金湯匙出生的。（Jenny was born）

___

5. 我抓到訣竅了。（hang）

___

6. 這超簡單的。（piece）

___

7. 我要休一年的假。（take）

___

8. 我要做的事一堆。（plate）

___

9. 你站在他的立場上想想。（Put yourself）

___

10. 南希是大嘴巴。（big）

___

解答 1

1) Expand your horizon.　2) Your mind is in the gutter!　3) I had a blast.　4) Jenny was born with a silver spoon in her mouth.　5) I got the hang of it.　6) It's a piece of cake.　7) I'm gonna take a year off.　8) I have a lot on my plate.　9) Put yourself in his shoes.　10) Nancy has a big mouth.

Exercise 2 依照句意填入正確答案。

1. 打破舊有框架

Think _____ the box

2. 恕我直言

With all _____

3. 打工

_____ job

4. 找到根本原因

_____ bottom of it

5. 熬夜

Pull an _____

6. 好的開始是成功的一半。

Well begun is _____ .

7. 你考慮看看。

_____ on it.

8. 說比做簡單。

It's easier _____ .

9. 太扯了！

You can't be _____ !

10. 你沒有選擇的餘地。

Beggars can't _____ .

解答 2

1) outside   2) due respect   3) Part-time   4) Get to the   5) all-nighter   6) half done   7) Sleep
8) said than done   9) serious   10) be choosers

231

EZ TALK

100+ 句學校沒教的英文慣用語：
秒讚口說考官高分表達，
躍升母語程度 English Speaker

作　　　者	：	Lora
譯　　　者	：	阿譯
責 任 編 輯	：	許宇昇／賴祖兒
封 面 設 計	：	謝捲子
內 頁 設 計	：	白日設計
文 字 排 版	：	簡單瑛設
行 銷 企 劃	：	陳品萱

發 　行 　人	：	洪祺祥
副 總 經 理	：	洪偉傑
副 總 編 輯	：	曹仲堯
法 律 顧 問	：	建大法律事務所
財 務 顧 問	：	高威會計師事務所

出 　　　版	：	日月文化出版股份有限公司
製 　　　作	：	EZ叢書館
地 　　　址	：	臺北市信義路三段151號8樓
電 　　　話	：	(02) 2708-5509
傳 　　　眞	：	(02) 2708-6157
網 　　　址	：	www.heliopolis.com.tw
郵 撥 帳 號	：	19716071日月文化出版股份有限公司

總 　經 　銷	：	聯合發行股份有限公司
電 　　　話	：	(02) 2917-8022
傳 　　　眞	：	(02) 2915-7212

印 　　　刷	：	中原造像股份有限公司
初 　　　版	：	2022年 5月
定 　　　價	：	380元
Ｉ Ｓ Ｂ Ｎ	：	978-626-7089-49-1

100+ 句學校沒教的英文慣用語：秒讚口說考官高
分表達，躍升母語程度 English Speaker/Lora 作；
阿譯譯 . -- 初版 . -- 臺北市：日月文化出版股份有
限公司 , 2022.05
　　面；　公分 . -- (EZ talk)
譯自 : 찐 미국 사람 영어회화
ISBN 978-626-7089-49-1 (平裝)
1.CST: 英語　2.CST: 慣用語
805.123　　　　　　　　　　　111002794

MEMO

MEMO

MEMO

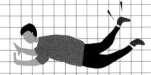

MEMO